A Chocolate Christmas

A Christmas Market Novel

The Tinsel Travelers Series
Book 1

Steena Holmes

Please note this was once called A Library of Christmas Memories for a short time in 2023.

Copyright © 2023 by Steena Holmes

All rights reserved.

No part of this book may be reproduced in any form or by any electronic or mechanical means, including information storage and retrieval systems, without written permission from the author, except for the use of brief quotations in a book review.

A Belgium Chocolate Christmas

Some Christmas trips should come with a warning label...

Every year the Tinsel Traveler friends visit Christmas markets in different countries. This year is Belgium.

Mara wasn't planning on going though, she was grieving the loss of her mother Stella. But her Tinsel Traveler friends - women who have become her family; Donna, Jo-Jo, Kat, Sandra, and Lucy, weren't leaving one of their own behind.

If it wasn't bad enough Mara had to be ready to leave in two days, Lucy gives her the first of a series of letters left by Stella, letters that reveal shocking discoveries and Mara questions if her whole life has been one lie after another.

With each letter Mara reads, Stella reveals another truth.

Amidst the twinkling lights of Brussels and Bruges, Mara looks to Lucy for answers, and it turns out visiting Belgium wasn't just about the lure of handmade crafts and the aroma of mulled wine, or even the amazing chocolate. The bed and breakfast they're staying at holds the key to Mara discovering more about her past and learning the truth the whole truth to who she really is.

And every Christmas trip must involve markets, carols, and of course chocolate!

During delicious chocolate walks and meanders through the Christmas Markets, not to mention tasting the different gluwein and endless hot toddies, Mara grapples with feelings of betrayal and forgiveness towards those she loves the most, she wonders if there are more secrets to come?

Explore fairy-tale Christmas Markets with *The Library of Christmas Memories*, the first book in The Tinsel Travelers Series, a new series that fans of Viola Shipman, Jenny Colgan, Rachel Hanna, and Mary Kay Andrews will enjoy.

A Special Thank You...

A very special thank you to those in my reader group (Steena's Secret Society) on Facebook! This book has been a long time coming, and you were always there rooting me on!

I have to give special thanks to those from my reader group for allowing me to use their name for characters in the story - with slight deviations! You are so appreciated! Special thanks to Sandra Haight, Amy Coats, Joanne Caldwell, Lola Herrerias, Shari Armon, Robin Lynn and Ken Batterson, and Donna Hepburn.

Thank you to Nancy Jean Rose for suggesting the name of the Wool Mitten Bookshop - it's absolutely perfect. And to Laurie, my #chocolateaddict sister, for exploring Belgium and Amsterdam with me and walking me through all the basics on working with chocolate.

Chris and Nenita Lindsay, what can I say but that I love you two!

Kelly Charron, Cindi Shroyer and Danielle Khuller - thank you for your keep eye, for giving your feedback, and for letting me bounce ideas off of you.

PS...All liberties taken regarding location of shops, residences, and experiences are purely mine.

A Note from Steena

I had so much fun writing this book - I know I probably say that about most of my novels, but this one is extra special. Why?

Every single experience, every secondary character, every place mentioned in this book is drawn from personal experience!

I'll explain more after you've finished reading the story...so don't skip that page!

All the chocolate, all the markets, all the fun things that happen...including the chocolate walks...it's all things I've done personally during my trips. While writing each scene, I would go through my photos and I was instantly brought back to my time there.

It's no secret that I love Bruges, Belgium, and so it was a delight to set most of this story in that town!

I also added Cochrane, Alberta, another town that I'm in love with. It's situated just outside of Calgary, Alberta (where I live) and has the cutest bookshop you'll ever find - it's called FOUND and you should look them up on Instagram!

Okay...before I say too much, enjoy the story!

Chapter One

Mara Pearce is three days shy of her forty-sixth birthday.

She's three days shy of a birthday she won't be celebrating, and she's completely fine with that.

So fine, in fact, that she'd be more than happy if she could forget her own birthday, but sadly, that's not a gift she can give herself.

Not yet. One day, for sure. She even knows when that day will come. Well, maybe not the exact day, week, or even month, but she can estimate that she will have forgotten most things about her life before she turns sixty, and she's completely fine with that.

Completely. Fine.

Until then, she has approximately fourteen more years of trying to forget a day she now hates with every single fiber of her being.

This year is going to be different. She's not sure how she feels about that.

Normally, around her birthday, she would be in Europe, exploring Christmas Markets with her travel friends, but not this year. Mom was always with her before, excited about exploring the markets, all the gluwein and gingerbread she could eat, and creating new memories.

Tomorrow, her mom would have turned sixty years young. They always shared their birthdays, being two days apart. For as long as Mara can remember, her mother wanted to visit the markets in Belgium for this specific birthday. They didn't make it last year. Of all the Christmas markets they'd been to over the years, Belgium was the one place they'd stayed away from for the one reason: it was Stella's trip.

As a group, they alternated their trips - every other year was Christmas in Europe, followed by something more local-ish - anywhere from an Alaskan cruise to a Mexico resort or even visiting well-known Christmas towns with the United States. When they went all depends on ticket prices. They would look for the cheapest tickets and go from there.

This year, they found dream prices to Amsterdam, and since it was a place they'd never been before, they all jumped at the tickets.

It was a dream trip, one for the memories, especially when it came to Stella, except now it's a trip that will never happen, not for her mother. Not for her, either.

Two weeks ago, Mara said goodbye to Stella, standing by her mother's casket until the sky turned a beautiful shade of evening rose pink, and numbly headed home to realize she was now alone.

She always knew one day she'd be an orphan.

She just never expected that day to happen so soon.

Dementia is a deadly weapon that destroys dreams and shatters hearts. She wouldn't wish it on her worst enemy, no matter what they'd done to her.

Watching her mother slowly lose herself was the hardest thing she'd ever done.

Surely, figuring out how to live the rest of her short life alone wouldn't be as hard.

She pulls herself out of her fog of depression and glances

around. She may be alone now, but she still has a life to live, and there's no better place than here.

Mara lives above a used bookshop. She not only lives above it, but she helps to run it in Cochrane, Alberta. The Wooly Mittens Bookshop is aptly named since Gus and Lily, the owners, also own a sheep farm, and they sell handmade mittens, toques, and scarves in the shop.

She loves this shop. It's a mixture of used and new, with titles combined on the shelves, so you can't tell the difference. There are enough nooks and crannies for people to sit, with antique chairs, old church pews covered in cushions, and even a hand-me-down large comfy chair where people can read for hours without noticing the time.

One of Gus's favorite things to do on weekends is to browse antique shops and garage sales for used furniture, fix them up with a fresh coat of paint or fabric, and then add it somewhere in the store. His favorite is old side tables, coffee tables, or even small kitchen tables where he can create book displays for people to browse as they walk through the store.

This store is more than just a brick-and-mortar shop. You walk in and know you're amongst friends. It's a place where you can sip coffee, meander through the shelves, chat with someone you've known most of your life, and even relax for a little while.

It's special. Unique. Not the type of shop you'd find in the city, which is something Mara really appreciates.

And right now, it looks like a Christmas fairytale.

The bookshelves are all covered in twinkling lights, a Christmas tree fills the front window and is decorated with bookish ornaments, Gus has festive music playing low in the background, and the store will soon smell like the warm apple cider warming in the crockpot.

"Got a few more boxes back here for you to shelve when you're done lallygagging up there," Gus calls out as he comes out from the back room, his gruff voice dripping with sarcasm.

She glances over her shoulder and catches the smile he's trying to hide. "Geesh, you're quite the hard master today, aren't you? What happened? Lily drink all the coffee or something?"

Gus shakes his head and mumbles something she can't quite make out.

"What's that?" Mara slips the last few books on her cart onto the shelves and heads back to the main desk.

"I said, the woman was out of the house faster than a bee in a bonnet, and all we had in the cupboard was that nasty instant garbage. I had to buy some of that fast food crap stuff instead, and I might as well as drink murky water," he complains in a huff.

He pushes a stack of books her way. "Figured you might want to read these first."

"Would you like me to make a fresh pot? I made a few cups worth earlier, but I drank it all. I could do with another cup myself," she offers.

Gus might come across as a grumpy old man, but everyone who knows him knows he's got the softest heart and hugs like a giant teddy bear. In fact, he dresses up as Santa every year and reads Christmas stories to the kids over the holidays.

"I wouldn't say no, that's for sure," he remains behind the desk and waits for her to look over the stack of five novels he set aside.

She can tell from the titles they're all holiday destination fiction novels, her favorite type of books to read. Give her a Christmas setting in a foreign destination; add a cafe, ski lodge, chocolate shop, or something else that's cute and quaint, with a little touch of romance, and she's lost. There's nothing more satisfying than curling up in one of the comfy chairs Gus has placed around the store and reading during their slow moments.

Although slow moments during the holidays are a rare thing.

"Oh, I haven't read any of these. When did they come in?" She didn't remember seeing them in their large stack of used books.

"Lily picked them up from someone in the city who had boxes of books in their garage." A frown on his face appears. "No book deserves to live in a box. They belong on a shelf for someone like you to come along and read."

Gus firmly believes in the power of books and how transformative they can be in the right hands. It's why he gives away books to every child who comes into the store as a gift during his Christmas readings.

The one thing he hates the most is to hear of books being boxed up and forgotten about.

"If you don't have room on your shelf for books, give them to someone who does," Mara parrots one of Gus's favorite sayings. He says it so often that they now have book bags and swag with the saying printed on them.

Customers love it, and personally, so does she. As a Christmas gift last year, Mara customized staff aprons with the saying placed beneath the store logo, and of course, Gus had been tickled pink. He always wears his, and now they give one out to customers in a monthly prize basket.

The bell over the door jingles, stealing Mara's attention from the books.

"Well, hello, you two," a warm voice greets them. "Please tell me you have coffee on, and it's extra strong?" Nenita Kahale walks in with open arms and wraps them around Mara.

"Coffee," Gus grumbles. "Guess I'll go make it since you'll be too busy gossiping now." He continues to grouse as he makes his way to the back, stopping first at the coffee counter to grab the empty decanter. "All out of regular creamer too, what, you drink it all and like a heathen, you don't replace it?" He shoots Mara a look before pushing the swinging door open.

Mara sighs while Nenita chuckles.

"Someone seems a little grumpy this morning," Nenita says.

"I think Lily had an early knitting class this morning, and you know how Gus is when he's out of his routine."

"He's like any other man, then. Be glad you don't have one to deal with."

"Ahh, but I do. I work with Gus every day, remember?"

Nenita sets a bag she'd been carrying on the counter and pulls out a container. "You know, besides offering coffee and cider to your customers, you should give them something to snack on as well," she opens the lid and reveals decorated Christmas sugar cookies. "I made extras and thought I'd bring them in. Didn't you used to have a cookie jar out once?"

A flood of memories rushes in, and Mara turns away to hide the sudden influx of swelling tears.

Her mom used to make cookies for the shop. Every Monday and Wednesday, she'd bake a few dozen assorted cookies, changing up the flavors each week. All of that changed a few years ago when dementia became a part of their lives. The last time her mother had made cookies, she'd almost started a kitchen fire.

"Oh honey, I'm so sorry," Nenita says as she rests her hand on Mara's shoulder. "I totally forgot."

Mara quickly wipes the evidence of tears from her cheeks and turns. "It's okay. I think I know where the cookie jar is. Let me grab it." She disappears down one of the book aisles and opens a storage closet. Sure enough, the jar is there. Complete with a hanging chalkboard label with Mom's handwriting on it.

She hesitates before reaching for it. Mom loved baking. She grew up working in a bakery and always said baking in a quiet kitchen was her version of heaven.

"It will get easier," Nenita says, appearing beside her. "The pain doesn't go away, but you find ways to get through the hard moments until the memories don't hurt as much."

Mara nods, unable to speak around the knotted bundle of tears caught in her throat.

Everyone says it will get easier, but they never tell her when that will happen.

Chapter Two

The grieving process, for her at least, started three years ago when they got the official diagnosis. Anticipatory grief, her counselor called it. Exhaustive grief is more like it.

Of all the people to understand, though, it's Nenita. Her own husband, Chris, is in the early onset stages of the disease, a disease Nenita is more than familiar with after losing her own father to it years ago as well.

They head over to the coffee bar where she washes out the jar in the small sink and hands it to Nenita to dry. There's a look on the woman's face that puzzles her.

Mara can't quite read Nenita today. She's cheerful and bubbly, like normal, but there's an underlying layer of tension, too. Something's up.

"How are you doing?" Mara asks.

"I'm fine, don't worry about me. Nothing a good cup of coffee can't fix." She says this last part a little extra loud.

"I'm coming, I'm coming," Gus yells. "Good coffee takes time, don't you know?"

They both chuckle a little. Nenita fills the jar with the cookies and writes the type on the chalkboard.

"I'll go see if he needs help," Mara says. She heads into the back just in time to see Gus pouring the fresh pot into the decanter.

"You make sure she doesn't drink it all, you hear?" He tells her. Mara ignores him, knowing full well he's being cankerous for the sake of it.

"She brought Christmas cookies."

One of Gus's eyebrows lifts up in surprise. "Well, in that case, she can drink as much as she wants. I can always make more," he says, handing her the decanter before searching the counter for his cup.

"Check the dishwasher," Mara tells him before returning to Nenita.

There are two mugs already waiting on the counter.

"Where is the flavored creamer?" Nenita asks. "Please tell me you're not all out?"

"Of our creamer? You know me better than that. I might not have refilled the one Gus uses, but I always make sure my creamer is there." Mara bends down to open the mini-fridge. She could have sworn she'd placed a new bottle of peppermint mocha there this morning.

"Looking for this?" Gus asks as he pushes open the door while holding a tray.

"How did that end up back there?" Mara went through her morning steps in her head. She made coffee, unboxed new donations left at the back door, counted the till, and then turned on the lights. She remembers seeing a container of creamer, but that was about it.

"Guess I meant to bring it out and forgot," Mara finally admits. One more forgetful thing to add to the list. She's keeping track now. How can she not?

"Don't stress about it. It's only creamer," Nenita says, squeezing her shoulder.

"So, what's going on this morning? Where is your husband, by the way?" Mara asks Nenita, who gives a slight eye roll at her question.

"He's probably sitting at the kitchen table, eating his bacon and eggs, enjoying being alone."

Mara might just be a coffee pourer and book finder, but she's pretty good at reading between the lines.

"Not a good day, huh?" Good days meant easy days. There aren't many easy days when taking care of someone with dementia.

Nenita snorts.

"His book came in if that helps?" Chris had placed an order for a photography book over a month ago. He's been in almost every day asking for it.

"I don't think that will matter," Nenita says. "He's not talking to me again. I swear, I totally forgot about the mood changes and how redonkulous they can get."

Holy hell and redonkulous are Nenita's two favorite words; hearing her sweet voice say them makes Mara smile every time.

"A silent Chris is a weird Chris." Mara takes the creamer from Nenita and pours a dash into her own mug. "I remember a few months ago, he came and sat in that corner chair, not saying a single word for two hours, and he drank a whole pot of decaf while at it."

Nenita's lips quirk. "Oh, that was the day I wouldn't let him wear his pink flamingo Panama pants outside when we had that freak snowstorm in September."

Pink flamingo Panama pants. Now, that's something you don't see every day.

"What set him off today?"

Nenita leans against the counter with her coffee mug between her hands. "He was looking for a photo we'd lost during our move when we downsized." She scrolls through her phone and finds the image, showing it to Mara.

"I can print that off," Mara offers. It's a photo of Chris and

Nenita standing in a footfall field. They were young, and the smiles on both their faces were full of laughter.

"Could you? My printer is out of ink, so that would be great, thank you." She glances down at the image. "That was our first date. The photographer asked us where we saw ourselves in five years, and Chris said in bed, with me beside him." Nenita's face blazed bright red as a blush crept along her skin.

Gus laughs. "That sounds like him."

"He said that on your first date?" Not that Mara is too surprised; one thing she's learned from knowing Chris Kahale, there's more below the surface than anyone expects.

"Right? The photographer caught the perfect moment, don't you think? His words registered, and that's when I knew I'd marry him. I've never regretted it, either." She sips at her coffee while gazing out the side window. "Even now, even knowing we'd end up here, I'd do it all over again. Just sooner so we could have created more memories together."

"Sooner?" Mara asks. "Didn't you guys get married right out of high school?"

Nenita nods. "Sure did. Okay, maybe not get married sooner, but I wish we'd met earlier."

"So, no regrets?" Mara asks, coming back to what Nenita had mentioned.

"I'm with the man I love. I'll steal as many moments with him as I can get."

Mara returns to the pile of books she'd started putting away earlier. "So about the cookies..." Maybe she can convince Nenita to bake them on a regular basis for them.

"Nope, not going to work. You won't side-track me that easily," Nenita says as she grabs a cookie from the jar. "How are you holding up?"

With her head bowed, she pretends to look through the titles on her cart, wishing she'd done a better job at hiding her feelings.

How is she holding up? Not very well at all, if she was going to be honest.

"Fake it till you make it, isn't that what they say?" Mara drops the book in her hands and rubs the back of her neck. "Tomorrow, Mom would have turned sixty. I was supposed to go to Amsterdam with the others and create memories I could share with Mom when I got back. I mean, I canceled my flight for obvious reasons, but, I think it hit me this morning just how much my life has changed in the past few months." She bites her lips and half turns to look out the front door. "I've never been one for change, you know that."

"No, you definitely are not. It's the fear of the unknown, right?" Nenita says, her voice as soft and gentle as a cashmere scarf. "What was that thing Stella always said?" Nenita taps a finger against her chin.

"Change can be happy," they say in unison.

"Mom painted that on a sign once when I was a kid."

Change and happiness are two describing words Mara's mother always embraced. But, when she turned fifty-seven, change became a tether, a weight, and finding happiness on a regular basis wasn't always easy. Not for her mom. Not for herself. The end came too quick, too. Quicker than she was ready for.

Choose happy, Mara, her mother's whispered words wrap around her in a warm hug.

Every night as a child, when her mother would tuck her into bed, gently kiss her forehead, she would whisper the same mantra - '*Choose happy, Mara. When you choose to be happy, nothing can stop you.*' She'd then ask where she found happiness, and when she was old enough to journal, she challenged her to write about every moment of happiness she found throughout the day.

Her mom kept one, too, and they would go through them together at night, sharing their day and remembering the moments.

Finding happiness with her mom was always easy.

Now that she's gone, Mara isn't sure anymore where to find those moments.

"I know you both used to go on these trips for your birthdays. I wish you hadn't cancelled it. Stella would have wanted you to go, you know that." Nenita gives her hand a squeeze.

"It wouldn't be the same. I'd only bring the others down. I think that maybe this is a year to skip birthdays," Mara says with a heaviness she wishes she didn't feel.

"Or, maybe it's the year to start creating new memories," Nenita says as she gives her a gentle squeeze. "You're not alone," she whispers into Mara's ear.

New memories. What a concept. For the past three years, all she'd focused on were the old memories, of living in the past with her mother, of strolling memory lane over and over and over again. Little by little, their lives revolved around the past, and she became disenchanted with the present.

"I made Mom a promise to learn to live life day by day, moving forward and not looking back again." She's honestly not sure how she can keep that promise, though. It feels hard. Harder than she expected.

The look of approval on Nenita's face tells her all she needs to know.

"And on that note...you go curl up in one of those chairs with your coffee while I finish putting these away before I get a tongue-lashing from Gus." She interjects a smile into her voice, a smile she doesn't feel.

Fake it till you make it, isn't that the saying?

She's been faking these smiles for a long, long time now. She should be a pro at it.

Chapter Three

"What are you still doing here?" Gus walks through the back doors and pulls out a seat at the table where Mara is going through their inventory lists. "Thought I told you to go for a walk or something. It's nice out. Take advantage of it while you can. It's not too often we get Chinooks like this," he continues as he slides the list she's looking at toward him.

"I'll go, eventually," Mara says, sliding the list back. He's right. She should head outside for a walk. Normally, this time of the year requires boots, winter jackets, scarves, and earmuffs. It's so nice out, she was tempted to open a window and would have if Gus wasn't around.

"I've already done inventory. Get out of here. You need some fresh air," Gus grumbles as he leans forward and plants his hand down, fingers spread across the sheet of paper.

"Gus..."

"You're off shift. I promised your mother I wouldn't let you lose yourself in work. Don't make me break that promise now." His gruff is softer, and the slight tilt of a smile playing with his lips helps somewhat.

Mara sighs. Getting lost in work is exactly what she wants to do, and making promises to a woman who wasn't going to remember that same promise was a waste of time. Gus is only saying it because he knows nothing else will work.

She pushes her chair back and fixes a firm frown on her face. "I'm going, but I'm not happy about it."

"Don't care if you're happy or not," Gus says. "Just go. I don't want to see your face again today, you hear me? Go bug someone else." He shoos me away like he's swatting after a fly.

"You're not being very nice, you know." She knows he loves her, but right now, his love feels a little tough.

She grabs her purse and heads out the door, unsure of where she's going.

She lives in one of the best small towns of Alberta, and when it comes to celebrating the holiday season, they're at the top of all those 'must visit' lists. Wreaths hang from every streetlight, lights wind through every fence post, planters are filled with winter shrubs, and the rustic vibe of the town is felt everywhere.

Over the years, one of Stella's favorite things to do was drive through the streets and see all the decorated houses. They'd fill their mugs with hot cocoa and slowly drive through town, whispering words of *ohh and ahh* along the way. This might be her first year she doesn't do that. Without her mom, it won't be the same this year.

She finds herself turning down First Street, a street full of restaurants, cowboy-themed bars, kitschy coffee shops, and her favorite diner - a hidden gem called Fence and Post.

The owners, Amy and Jeff Coats, turned what was once a regular diner into something extra special. With the outdoor facade, something that could be found in any old Western movie, the inside is as cute. She hasn't been in it since Amy decorated the place for the holidays, but she's seen photos. She stayed with the whole rustic Christmas design, which is perfect.

Gus told her to go for a walk, but sitting with Amy, and eating a bowl of her chicken stew sounds about perfect right about now.

Mara opens the door to the restaurant and almost closes it when she sees the place half full.

Maybe this wasn't the best idea. She should go home instead and order in. A quiet night, with no one else around, just her and an empty house. She's got to get used to it at some point, right?

"Mara!" Her name is called across the floor, and she looks up to see Amy waving at her from the counter.

Well, that's it now - there's no way she can leave.

She finds an empty table and scoots around so she's sitting on the bench with her back against the wall and plays with the cute reindeer salt and pepper shakers on the table.

"I was just thinking about you," Amy says as she pulls out a chair and plops down. "How are you doing?" Her hand reaches out and gently enfolds Mara's in a motherly gesture.

Tears immediately spring to Mara's eyes. This was eventually going to stop hurting, right?

"Oh, honey," Amy says, tears filling her own eyes. There's a sense of compassion and safety in Amy's presence, and until this exact moment, Mara didn't realize just how much she needed her friend.

"The place looks amazing, by the way," Mara wipes at the tears, desperate to focus on something, anything other than her grief. "I especially love that tree with all the snowflakes and farm decor. It's...cute."

"It's kitschy and goes with the theme. The Cochrane Gazette is coming in this weekend to take photos. Listen, I have an idea, and you're not allowed to say no, okay?" Amy pauses, her eyes sparkling with sudden mischief. "Things are about to get crazy here, it's always chaotic during the holidays, so tomorrow, you and I are going to play hooky and run away for the day. How does that sound?" Amy leans back in her chair, throwing her arms in the air to emphasize how great her idea is.

A whole list of reasons why it wasn't a good idea settles on the tip of Mara's tongue, but for some reason, she can't say them.

She promptly closes her mouth, which only adds to the grin on Amy's face.

"Right? It sounds amazing and exactly what we need. I know I could use a break from this place, and I know you can use a break from everything, too. And don't worry, I've already told Gus I'm stealing you, so he won't put up too much of a fuss."

"Oh, he'll fuss all right," Mara says.

"True. I swear that man loves to make mountains out of molehills for no other reason than to cause a scene just for the sake of it. I need this day, and so do you."

Rather than argue, which she knows will do no good, she might as well go with the flow of things. Amy is right. Getting away for the day will be nice. "So, where are we headed?"

"It's a secret." From the glean in her eye and the excited smile growing on Amy's face, Mara knows right away where they're going.

"It's Banff, isn't it?" She struggles to roll her eyes. Amy's favorite place to get away is to the quaint mountain town, specifically the Banff Springs Hotel Spa where she'll buy a day pass and soak in the pools, hot tubs and indulge in a massage and facial.

"How did you know? You can't say no because I've already purchased a package for the two of us. You know you could use a massage, right? Besides, the hotel is amazing during the holidays. No one does Christmas better. And when was the last time you spent the day taking care of yourself instead of someone else?"

"Who else was going to take care of Mom?"

"I didn't mean that, and you know it." There's a slight scolding to Amy's tone.

"I know, I'm sorry." She takes a moment to breathe through all the emotions wanting to come to the surface. She's sad, angry, frustrated, and even feeling a tad bit judged. None of that is Amy's fault, and it's not right to take it out on her.

Maybe coming here was a mistake. She should have headed to

one of the walking paths located throughout town and just let herself feel.

Feel what, now that's the question. When it comes to the grieving process, she seems to be alternating between the sadness of losing her mom and being alone, to guilt for feeling a semblance of relief that the waiting game is over, and she can finally move on with her life.

She can move on while her mother now lies in her grave. She's the worst daughter ever, and yet, she knows her mom wouldn't want her to lose herself in the grief either.

"I'll pick you up at nine. I'll even bring coffee, all you need to bring is your bathing suit and flip-flops and be ready for some pampering, okay? Oh, and I'll have one of the drivers drop off dinner for you tonight, that way it won't get cold as you walk home. Let me guess…chicken stew?"

Mara smiles. "Am I that predictable?"

"It's my go-to comfort food. Listen, I'm not taking no for an answer, Mara."

Mara glances around and notices that the place is fuller than before. "I'll let you get back to work," she says.

"Mara?" One word, but the question is there in the tone.

"Oh, all right. How can I say no to a day of pampering, especially when it's a birthday gift." She lets a smile light along her face and gives her friend a quick hug. "I'm so glad you're in my life," she whispers past the lump of tears in her throat.

"Oh honey, I love you, I hope you know that. I know it's hard right now, but you aren't alone, I promise you." Amy lightly rubs her back, a true mothering gesture, and Mara does everything she can not to cry.

She quickly puts the sunglasses on and heads outside, keeping her face down, so no one passing by would see her swollen eyes. She's not exactly what you'd call a cute crier. Her nose gets all red, the bags under her eyes double in size, and the red splotches on her skin can be seen from miles away.

What she needs right now is to head home, curl up in her reading chair with one of the books Gus found for her, eat the stew, and then devour one of the many tubs of ice cream in her freezer.

She takes the long way back to her house, walking a few extra blocks to get her steps in, and checks her phone for any messages.

She groans at all the missed messages. Some from friends wanting to check in, but the most are from her travel group - The Tinsel Travelers.

They're a group of six women, all ranging from the ages of forty-five to sixty, with Mara being the youngest. They met years ago through a small group tour to Paris and became fast friends. They've traveled to Italy, Greece, the UK, France, and even Germany a few times. It's been a few years though, since they traveled as a group. This would have been the first one since the lockdown.

Life has a habit of getting in the way of fun, sometimes.

Sandra: *So, are we still on for 7:30pm? Mara...don't ignore this.*

Kat: *Mara...girl, are you seeing this? 7:30pm, chat time, I've got news!*

Kat: *Everyone accepted my video request except for Mara. Girl... you can not miss our call, got it?*

Kat: *Mara...MARA...I'm going to call you soon if you don't respond.*

She'd totally forgotten about the video call tonight. She'd got the video request a few days ago but promptly forgot about it.

Sorry guys, I flaked out on this. I'll be there. You must all be so excited for your trip! See you soon. Mara adds a smiling emoji to her message, then pockets her phone before it floods with more messages.

This group has been her lifesaver over the past few years. Each friendship is unique and personal, and she wouldn't have been able to get through her mom's sickness without their support.

Especially Lucy Beckers.

A Belgium Chocolate Christmas

Originally Lucy and Stella had hit it off, both being close in age. On most of the tours they did, Stella and Lucy were considered the mother hens, with Lucy being the one to take care of organizing everyone's itinerary, while Stella took care of everything else. Stella was a hoverer, a caregiver. The best mom a girl could have.

Since then, Lucy has been a constant presence in Mara's life, so much so that she even came to help take care of Stella, giving Mara a little break here and there.

Lucy might have started off as Stella's friend, but she quickly became Mara's family. Their relationship even morphed into something stronger than friendship, for which Mara is so grateful. Lucy isn't a substitute mother, she's more like an older sister, one Mara leans on when things get to be too much.

She feels her phone vibrate and pulls it out. She silenced notifications from almost everyone since the funeral, but not for Lucy.

Lucy: *We need to chat before the video call. Are you free around seven?*

Mara sends her a thumbs-up emoji, then quickly puts her phone away as she crosses the street.

When she arrives at the bookstore, she heads to the side where her private door is located. There, waiting for her is a box. She lifts it and is surprised at the weight.

Once she carries it upstairs and plants it on her kitchen table, she opens it only to find another box inside - with a note taped to it.

Do not open until the video call. On the note are drawings of balloons, hearts, and even a cake with candles.

She recognizes the handwriting of Donna Hempburn, and her heart melts.

Donna remembered her birthday. For some reason, this simple act brings tears to her eyes, which is odd because it's not like this is a surprise. Donna sends everyone birthday gifts, and Christmas and just because gifts.

She takes a photo of the unopened second box and sends it to Donna.

Not opened...but thank you! xoxoxo

Three little dots appear, then disappear, then reappear.

Donna: Like I'd forget! Don't open it till we're all on the call. Chat soon. Love you!

She's tempted...oh, she's so very tempted. Mara isn't one who likes surprises too much. When she was younger, she found every single gift her mom would hide away for her birthday or for Christmas. It wasn't that she needed to know, it was more the anticipation of what the secret could be that got to her. She'd try every year not to look for the spots, and every year, until her twelfth birthday, she'd give in.

On her twelfth birthday, her mom caught her snooping and promptly returned all the gifts. The only thing she got that year was a birthday cake and a card. It was a hard lesson to learn but learn it she did.

So, instead of opening the gift, she opts to open a new container of ice cream, carrying it with her into the living room. Dessert before dinner is a thing.

She picked up the top book from the stack she'd brought up earlier, but not before setting the alarm on her clock.

Her phone is filled with preset alarms. She lived by them to help with her mother's medications and appointments. Setting the alarms has become a habit, one she uses all the time now, even for little things - like not missing the chat tonight.

It wouldn't be the first time, if she did. It certainly won't be the last, either.

Everyone says that her lack of memory is normal, especially with the stress she's been under the past few years. Even her doctor has told her not to be concerned...yet.

It's the yet that has her worried.

Chapter Four

At seven on the dot, Lucy calls just as Mara pours some chocolate Bailey's into her hot mocha.

As the video opens, she sees Lucy sitting there, sipping what looks to be a cup of coffee.

"Great minds and all that," Mara says as she takes her own sip.

"Yeah, but yours is the full deal, right, lucky duck? At my age, the only time I can drink the real deal is first thing in the morning. Otherwise, my whole sleeping schedule is messed up."

"You're not that old, Lucy."

"I'm old enough, love, I'm old enough." The twinkle in Lucy's eyes shows just how young the woman truly feels. "How are you holding up?"

Mara dips her head and stares at the cup in her hand.

"I don't think I knew what to expect, to be honest," Mara says. "Mom and I would talk about it, what life would be like once she was gone, but..." she falters, unable to finish.

"It's never what you expect. How can it be? Talking about it is one thing. Living it is another. Your mother knew it wouldn't be easy, but I want you to remember, you're not alone." The sincerity in Lucy's voice hits Mara with all the right notes, and she can barely see from the tears gathering in her eyes.

"Do you remember that booklet of Moms? The one she wrote her wish list in? I went looking for it the other day, but I couldn't find it." Mom generally kept it by her chair in the living room. She loved to watch travel shows and take notes of places to go and things to do.

"I remember. We managed to check some things off."

"I can't find it. I wanted to relive some of those memories, you know? Like how she wanted to swim in the ocean, go snorkeling with the turtles, spend a day touring all the bakeries in the area…"

"She got to do almost everything, didn't she?"

Mara nods. "Except one."

"Belgium," Lucy says, reading her mind.

"It's the one trip she wanted to do. She's already been to Paris, Italy, Germany…she traveled most of Europe when she was younger. Of all the places she wanted to return, it was Belgium, for some reason."

"She had a reason for that," Lucy said, a little bit cryptic.

Mara leans back, intuitively knowing there's more that Lucy needs to say.

"Back in the beginning, before her memory really started going, your mother and I had a good chat. Do you remember when I came down for the weekend while you joined the other girls in Vegas? That was probably one of the best weekends we'd had together in a long time."

"Mom had such a good time with you," Mara says, recalling how vibrant and alive her mother was when she returned home. She looked restful and peaceful. Mara mentioned the change but all Stella said was that her heart was lighter, and she was okay with what was coming.

She might have been, but Mara wasn't.

"That was a good weekend for both of us. We had a lot to get off our chests, a lot of things that needed to be said," Lucy pauses, a soft smile resting on her face. "It was a time we both needed. But we talked about Belgium, and how she knew she would never get there. That bothered her more than I expected, to be honest."

"Really? She used to tell me the best chocolates were in Belgium. She said of all the countries she's been, nothing compares, and you know how Mom was with her chocolate."

"I also know how you are with your chocolate," Lucy teases.

"Like mother like daughter. It's a family thing," Mara says.

"Yes, yes, it is." There's something in Lucy's voice that Mara catches but can't quite make out. Wistfulness? Sadness?

"That weekend, we did something, your mother and I. It's meant as a surprise, and it comes at the best timing. Do me a favor? In the bottom drawer of your china cabinet is an envelope with my name on it. Will you go get it?"

"What did you do?"

"Just go get it, woman, please."

Mara gets up and heads to the kitchen, where Mom's antique china cabinet is. She pulls out the sticky bottom drawer, having to see-saw its way open. There are a lot of things in this drawer, but an envelope with Lucy's name on it isn't one of them.

"Are you sure it's in here?" She calls out.

"Check under the photo albums," Lucy says.

There, on the left, is a stack of photo albums Mara had printed one year as a gift for Mom. They were yearly albums with photos from her phone that she'd taken from their road trips and adventures. Her mom loved these albums, and for the longest time, she'd look through them on a regular basis until there was one time she started ripping out the pages because she didn't recognize the people in the images.

She didn't recognize herself or even her daughter.

Mara cried herself to sleep that night, sobbing into her pillow, recognizing they'd crossed another bridge with the horrific disease.

Sure enough, as she pushes the albums to the side, she notices a big brown envelope with Lucy's name on it.

"If your name is on it, why did you leave it here? Why not take it with you after the funeral?" Mara asks as she returns to her seat.

"Because it's not meant for me," Lucy says. "It's for you, but we didn't want you to open it until it was time. It was your mom's idea to put my name on it. I think she knew even if you had found it, you wouldn't look inside."

Now she's intrigued.

"Happy birthday," Lucy says with a softness in her voice.

Mara rips the flap open, giving herself a tiny paper cut on her index finger. She pulls out her mom's wish list booklet, the same one she's been looking for, as well as a stack of printed paper.

"What's all this, Lucy? What's going on?"

Lucy doesn't say anything, but even if she had, Mara is too engrossed in reading the note left for her even to hear what Lucy has to say.

Dear Mara,

Happy birthday, love. My favorite time of the year is Christmastime. Not just because we would celebrate our birthday all month long, or because of the Christmas markets, but because you were the best gift I could ever have gotten for my birthday. I have one last birthday wish that I hope you can grant...go to Belgium for me, please. It's a beautiful place to be during the holidays. Eat all the chocolate. Drink all the gluhwein. Bring back more mugs from the markets. Take all the photos. Make all the memories you and I were supposed to make. Do this for me.

I love you, baby girl.

Mom

What? Why? How...she's lost for words to explain what she's reading.

"When I came to visit your mom," Lucy explains, "she wrote a bunch of letters to you, letters she didn't want you to read until after she was gone. She knew she'd never see Belgium again herself, but she wanted you to. And it's perfect timing since the girls are going there this year, don't you think?"

A Belgium Chocolate Christmas

Mara glances at the letter in her hand. "So this is purely..."

"Coincidental? Crazy, right? Or maybe it's meant to be. There should be something else in there..."

Struggling to comprehend what Lucy is saying, she flips through the papers, and sure enough, there's a printout for a flight, with her name of it, leaving in two days for Amsterdam. "Lucy? What - no, I can't...I'm not...I can't go on this trip. They leave in a few days. I've got work and..."

"Of course, you can go," Lucy says as if the answer is obvious.

Not without Mom.

"I don't have the money, and I can't take more time off work..."

"It's all paid for, and Gus already knows all about it."

"But..." Mara struggles with the idea that she's actually going to Belgium with the girls.

"You know your mother would want you to go. She says it's her wish, doesn't she? She had no idea that the girls would be going this year, but you know she wouldn't want you to miss out, not because of her, and certainly not because of her death. The girls and I had this planned for a while, ever since you said you were canceling your flight. Listen, everything is planned, so all you need to do is go and enjoy."

Enjoy? While she's grieving? How is that even possible?

"What about you?"

"I'll sit this one out. I'd originally planned to stay behind with your mom, so I never bought a ticket. But that's okay. Belgium was your mother's trip, not mine."

"I really don't think—"

"Of course, you are going to go. You've got two days to pack and plan, which is plenty of time."

Two days? She can't...

"Lucy, I chatted with Stephanie a few days ago. She never said a word." In fact, they talked about everything but this upcoming trip. Stephanie has been the Tinsel Travelers travel agent for as long as they've been together. In fact, Mara hasn't booked a trip without Stephanie's help one way or another for years. With all the mishaps that can happen while traveling, it's always nice to know there's someone who can take care of the details when problems arise.

"Of course, she wouldn't. She knew this was a surprise."

Mara sits back in her chair with a thump. She reaches for her cup and wishes she'd poured more Bailey's into the cup. This is all a little too much.

"I wish..." She struggles with the words lumped together in her mouth. "I wish you were coming too." She'd never traveled without her mother. In fact, since Lucy came into their lives, she'd actually never traveled without her mother and Lucy. This trip wouldn't be the same without her.

"Take lots of photos and share them online for me, will you? You'll have a good time, I know it. The girls will take care of things."

"I'm really leaving in two days?" She's seriously struggling to process all of this.

"You really are. The girls will tell you all about your trip tonight, but honestly, go with the flow and take it all in. Belgium is beautiful during the Christmas season. I'm not sure if Amsterdam has any markets, but still, that will be a beautiful city to explore with all the lights and such. I think Kat is in charge of the chocolate walks. She's made maps of all the best shops to visit and everything."

An alarm sounds, giving her a five-minute reminder for the call with the others.

"Breathe, Mara. Your mom wants you to go to Belgium for her, so that's what you are going to do, okay? Now, I need to get off this call and empty my bladder before we chat with everyone else. Love you."

Just like that, Lucy ends out of the video call, leaving Mara to sit there, staring at the blank screen, trying to take it all in.

Chapter Five

"Hello, gorgeous. Hey there, girl, happy early birthday."

"Mara...earth to Mara, hello..."

Mara finally snaps out of the cloud her mind is lost in and sees the images of her best friends on her computer screen.

Kathleen/Kat Graham, Sandra Height, Donna Hempburn, and Joanna/Jo-Jo Coldwell all sit there, each of them holding a glass in their hand, all of them with huge smiles on their faces. It is so good to see them. Even though they were all here for Mom's funeral service, hearing their voices, seeing the love in their eyes, it's exactly what she needs right now.

She just doesn't remember joining the call.

In fact, she doesn't remember much other than the bombshell of news Lucy threw her way earlier.

"Hey guys, sorry. I'm kind of in shock right now. Lucy just told me what's happening." Mara picks up her coffee as a slow smile starts to grow.

"Hey, where is Lucy?" Kat asks. "She is joining us, right?" Kat is the organizer of the group, the one who usually finds them cheap flights, and works with Stephanie, their travel agent, to get the flights and hotels all arranged. And even though each person in the group gets to organize their own trips, Kat is usually on hand to help.

Mara nods. "She had to run to the bathroom and probably refill her coffee."

"Okay, you guys, it's trip time. Is everyone ready?" Jo-Jo squeals in delight, her short bob bouncing as she does a little dance in her seat. "Bring on the Christmas Markets, the music, and the shopping."

Jo-Jo's energy wraps around Mara like a warm hug.

"This is going to be so fun," Donna says. "Now, Mara, where is that gift I sent? You didn't open it yet, did you?

"I was tempted," Mara says as she leans out of the view of the camera to slide the box closer. She holds it in front of her and starts opening it, her mind all mushy with feels.

"You're going to love it," Sandra says, her voice alight with laughter.

Mara closes her eyes for a second, taking in the warmth and energetic vibe she's getting from her friends. Having them in her corner, she doesn't feel as alone.

She opens the box and pulls out one wrapped item after another. Each is labeled with numbers.

"Open number one first," Donna dictates. When Mara looks up at the screen, all the women are leaning in close to their cameras, excited smiles on their faces.

"What did you guys do?"

"It's your birthday, and you're headed on a big trip. What did you think we would do?"

"Considering I didn't know I was going on a big trip until about...fifteen minutes ago, I don't know..."

She opens the first gift, and it's a container of packing cubes. The second is a toiletries kit where she can add her own shampoo and soap to the containers. Next is a portable phone charger, one that's small and light enough not to bulk up her purse and the next gift is actually a new travel purse.

"You guys," Mara's eyes fill with tears.

"Now you can throw out your old stuff," Donna says.

She proceeds to open a gift with a beautiful blue silk scarf inside that she'll know she'll always treasure and finally, there's a new travel journal.

On all their trips, Mara always brought a new notebook. She loved to take notes about their travels, where they went, where they shopped, what they ate…everything was documented.

She breathes in deep and lets all of this sink in.

"I'm going to Belgium," she says.

"You are. We all are. It's going to be so amazing." Donna says. Donna Hempburn is the second oldest of the group, and she's quite the mother hen. She has four children of her own and is married to the love of her life. They live on a farm in upper state New York, and she's the type of woman who brings her crochet hook and wool with her on flights.

A ding announces Lucy's arrival to the group chat. "Hey beautiful women, what have I missed?"

"Oh, just the fact we're all going on a trip, finally! Do you know how long it has been since we were all traveling together?" Donna's joyous smile quickly disappears. "Oh my god, that sounded horrible. Mara, I'm so sorry…"

Mara shakes her head. "Don't apologize. It's true. If I didn't stay behind with Mom, then Lucy did. But, Donna, Lucy isn't coming on this trip."

"Oh, yes, she is." Donna counters.

"Oh, no, I'm not." Lucy counters. "You guys have fun, though. I can't wait to live vicariously through all your photos." The smile on her face doesn't hold one hint of sadness at not joining them, which Mara finds surprising.

"Um, Lucy," Kat says, clearing her throat. "You are coming, hun. Check your email - I forwarded you your flight info." A twinkle appears in Kat's eyes, while a frown appears on Lucy's.

"What did you do?"

"This trip wouldn't be the same without you," Sandra pipes up. She swipes at her bangs to get them out of the way. "We all pitched in and took care of your flight and hotel costs. Merry early Christmas!"

"Oh, no, you didn't."

"Oh, yes, we did," Kat, Sandra, Donna, and Jo-Jo say in unison.

Mara giggles. "This is going to be so good," she says, tears filling her eyes yet again. "Tomorrow is, would have been, Mom's birthday," she says softly. "This is the perfect way to celebrate it, don't you think? For all of us to go to the one place she had on her list but never made it to?"

"There's no other way. Are you going to be okay tomorrow? You won't be alone, right?" Sandra asks.

Mara leans back with a sigh. "I'll be okay. Amy Coats, you all remember her? She owns the Fence and Post Diner? She's stealing me away, and we're having a spa day."

"Oh, that will be nice and something your mother would have loved," Lucy says. "Do you guys remember that hotel in Paris that had that spa in the basement? What was it called again?"

"La Maison Favart." Kat says without hesitation.

"Oh, I loved that hotel. Next time we go to Paris, we have to go back." Sandra swipes at her bangs again. "Augh, you guys, next time I ask if I'd look good with bangs, tell me no. I hate them." Sandra Height is one of the most personable women Mara has ever known. She's kind-hearted, soft-spoken, and, what you see is what you get kind of person. She lost her husband a few years ago and has been trying to live outside her comfort box ever since. Apparently, getting bangs was another not-so-successful step.

"I'll bring some cute clips you can use to hold them back off your face," Jo-Jo offers.

"I agree with that hotel. It was probably my favorite out of all our trips," Lucy says. "Especially that spa area, with those vaulted ceilings and all that stonework, it was like being in a luxury cave you never wanted to leave. Your mother loved going down to the hot tub and sneaking a glass of champagne with her."

"Was that the champagne that we brought back from Veuve Clicquot?" Donna asks.

"Only the best champagne ever." Jo-Jo holds up a champagne flute. Ever since that trip, it's the only kind she'll drink. Joanne is a socialite from New York City, and she recently got married for the fourth time. She's nothing you'd expect her to be and yet everything you need her to be. She's bright and bubbly, with a carefree attitude that attracts almost everyone around her. She's petite with what she'd call a fluffy hourglass figure and has more money than she lets on. She loves the fine life and has no qualms about letting people know.

"Oh, I don't know, I think I've had better since, but...it was good champagne, that's for sure." Donna winks into the camera. "I think we should test that, though...maybe we could have a champagne night video chat and taste test different bottles. I saw this place online where you can buy a sample kit."

"Oh, I love that idea. Although, it would be better if we were all together in person." Jo-Jo says.

"I don't want to wait that long. How about we do it right before New Year's? I'll take care of getting you all the kits. My Christmas gift to you all." Donna says as she looks down at something. "I'm making a note of it, and no one is backing out, you hear? Not even you, Lucy."

"Champagne really isn't my thing, love, you know that."

A bevy of complaints arise. "I seem to recall you loving the champagne just as much as Stella did," Jo-Jo says.

Lucy rolls her eyes and makes a long, dramatic sigh. "Fine, You're right, I do. I'm in."

"Um, can I ask about this trip? I mean, since I'm now coming, I'd love to know what's happening, pretty please?" Mara asks, looking directly at Kat since she knew she'd have the answers.

"Well," Kat says with a growing grin, "I've been working with

Stephanie to make this a trip I know Stella would love. Some of it I want to keep as a surprise, though, if that's okay. But we're all flying into Amsterdam, and we'll spend a day there before taking the train to Brussels, where, of course, we're going to start off with a chocolate walk and visit a Christmas Market or two."

"So we're staying in Brussels for a few days?"

Kat's eyes twinkle. "I've got it all planned, Lucy, don't you worry! We're each sharing a room, but we all have our own beds. Stephanie says exploring Belgium via train is easy, and we'll be going to all the best markets before coming home. I promise we'll be tired of the markets and full of chocolate by the time we leave."

Following the video chat with everyone, Mara takes all the papers from the envelope and retreats to her couch. She looks around the room, and the weight of the quiet, especially after the video chat, hits her.

"I should get a cat when I get back."

She goes through all the paper that was in the envelope and comes across another one addressed to her.

She recognizes her mother's scribbly scrawl and her hands shake a little as she holds it.

Her lips quiver as she stares at her mother's handwriting. She wants to open it, to read whatever it is her mom has to say, but at the same time, she doesn't want to lose this feeling of closeness with her either.

Right now, the letter can say anything. It can be a set of instructions for the trip, or a gentle walk through their life together. It can be all the things she'd wished she'd said before she died, or it could be gibberish of disjointed memories.

Girding herself to receive whatever is inside this envelope, Mara slowly opens it and immediately drops the paper on her lap as a large sob tears through her.

Chapter Six

Dear Mara,

It feels weird to be writing a letter to you that I know you won't read for a few years (hopefully a lot of years, but we know that probably won't happen). There are things I need to tell you, things I need to share, but I've been to chicken too do it in person.

I need to tell you though, before I forget the words I want to say. That scares me more than anything.

Yes, your mother, scared. I'm scared about what my life is going to be like, how it's going to affect you, but most of all, I'm scared to tell you something I should have confessed a long time ago.

You're going to be angry with me, and I'm sorry for that.

Angry that I never told you the truth. Angry that I'm not around to explain things. Angry that I can't answer the million questions I know you're going to have.

It's okay to be angry with me, Mara. Even with that anger, I know you still love me.

Just as I have always and will always love you.

Lucy is going to give you this letter before you head to Belgium, whenever that is - but I hope it's during one of the market trips so you aren't alone. I also hope Lucy goes with you. I had hoped we'd go together. Belgium changed my life. I know it's going to change yours. Not just because Belgium during the holidays is magical and not because I've always said real Belgium chocolate is like none other, but because I've kept a secret from you that can only be explained in Belgium.

Cryptic. I know. I imagine you're rolling your eyes at me right now.

I'm not going to lie, writing these letters and not telling you in person, that's the easy way out.

I hope you'll be with the girls on this trip. I hope that includes Lucy. She has her own reasons for not wanting to go to Belgium. She's part of our story in a way, and I want her to be there to share that story with you.

Here's what I've been too afraid to tell you: your father was from Belgium.

I have a lot of things to apologize for. I'm sorry I never told you about your father. I'm sorry I told you he died before you were born. I'm sorry I lied and stole memories that could have been yours.

It was easier, though. My heart was broken because he didn't choose me. He didn't even choose you. He chose his family, and I couldn't forgive him for that.

I still can't.

Whatever anger you feel toward me, I promise you, my anger toward him is stronger.

I say I wish I were there to explain everything in person, but the fact I'm making Lucy wait to give you this says that's all just a lie. I'm sorry for not being honest, for keeping this lie from you. This won't be the only letter. I'm trying to imagine what needs to be said with each new thing you learn and I'll probably bungle things up in ways only I can.

Can I ask one thing of you? Not to be mad at Lucy for any of this. All of this is on me. She has always disapproved of my decision to not tell you the truth, but you know me: I'm not called Stubborn Stella for nothing.

Now, about the Christmas Markets in Belgium and why this was something I wanted to do when I was sixty. A long time ago, I made a wish with your father, that we no matter where we were, we would return to Belgium for my sixtieth birthday and explore the markets. I don't remember why we made this wish, maybe it was because my own mother never reached sixty and I said I needed to make it a special year, or something. But a wish was made and it's a wish I've always kept close to my heart, for one reason or another.

So go. Enjoy wandering Brussels, get lost in Bruges, drink all the apple cider and spiced wine you can stomach and don't forget to bring home the mugs.

Make memories for both of us, memories you'll be able to hold on to and cherish before it's too late.

Have an extra piece of the good chocolate everywhere you go for me, please?

One thing I want you to know and always remember: I love you, Mara-mine.

I'm sorry for keeping so many secrets from you. I'm sorry for making decisions that impacted your life in ways I never understood. I'm sorry that I'm not there in person to explain things to you.

The journey you're about to go on, I hope, will bring some clarity and closure.

Whatever you find out, I want you to know that through it all, from the moment I found out that I was pregnant, all I've ever wanted was to be your mother.

I am so proud of you, for the woman you are, and I'm so thankful for all the memories we have together.

Now it's time to create some new ones.

Love, Mom

Chapter Seven

After reading her mom's letter, Mara spent a good portion of the evening trying to get in touch with Lucy, but the woman evaded all her calls and texts and has yet to reply to her emails.

Her mom can't just drop a bomb like that, telling her about her father and not giving any other information. And what story does Lucy have to tell that she hasn't already told?

Stella said she wrote the letters early on, back when they first got the diagnosis, but Mara has to disagree. She had to have written these afterward. There are so many holes in between the sentences, so many left out portions, and what feels like unfinished thoughts that lucidity can't have been in Stella's grasp.

Why would her mother bring up her father now, of all times?

A father she's never known. A father she's never thought of.

She always thought that particular parental figure was dead, and that was it - Stella would never expand on that, she'd never tell her stories about him, so throughout the years, Mara had no choice but to make her own.

He was a one-night stand while her mom was on her year-long Europe trip before her twentieth birthday, and that was that.

For all these years, she's been okay with that.

A Belgium Chocolate Christmas

When Amy came to pick her up this morning, she'd been a little quiet. When she saw the coffee waiting for her in the car, she almost cried.

That's a lie. She did cry. She cried as she sipped that coffee, cried as she held the warm cup between her hands, and continued to cry as they drove through the backroads, taking in the gorgeous snow-capped mountains ahead of them.

"Are you ready to tell me what's wrong?" Amy asks once they're back on the highway, her voice soft and warm, everything Mara needs at this moment.

One blubbery word at a time, it all comes out, from the surprise trip to the equally surprising letter. By the time they pull up to the Banff Springs Hotel, all the tears have dried up, and she feels a little lighter from sharing the heavy load. Amy never said much. She listened, she asked questions to clarify things, but she gave Mara the space to say everything she needs to say.

That's one thing she appreciates the most about Amy.

The hotel is amazing any time of the year, but during the holidays, it's spectacular. Known as the Castle in the Rockies, the Banff Springs Hotel gushes with elegance and ornate simplicity. From its hanging wreaths to its dangling lights, the plethora of Christmas trees around every corner, and the mouthwatering scent of apple cider…the hotel paints a picture of a warm Christmas hug.

In the lobby is a huge tree that shines bright, but the main attraction is the replica castle made entirely out of gingerbread and icing. Mara makes sure to take photos and send them to the Tinsel group with the hashtag #nexttripidea?

They make their way down a tree-lined hall where lighted garlands cover each archway and head straight to the spa, where they sign in, get changed, and wait for their massage dressed in oversized white bath robes while sipping cucumber water and nibbling on sugar cookies. When it's finally their turn for their massage, they make their way down another small hallway and come to a large room where two massage beds are set up.

"Try to enjoy this, okay, Mara? Your body needs it." Amy shrugs off her bathrobe and hangs it up on a waiting hook.

They're having a friends massage, and while Mara knows she's supposed to be relaxed, she can't. Her muscles are wound up too tight, and she feels more stressed than anything else.

Mara reaches out and gives her friend's hand a tight squeeze. "Thank you for this," she says.

"I've got you." It's a promise Amy has made since the beginning, and it's a promise Mara knows her friend will never break.

"I still can't believe you are headed to Europe tomorrow," Amy says, her voice muffled beneath a warming towel on her face.

"I'm so not prepared for this. You know me, it takes me months to plan for one of our big trips. I can't believe Lucy and the others planned all this in advance and never said anything."

"Deep down, you know you wanted to go on the trip. I think it's sweet that Lucy was going to stay with your mom if she were still here. You're going to enjoy it, you know that, right?"

"Well, I'm not sure I do. How can I enjoy it after all of this? Besides, this was her trip, something she wanted to do. How am I supposed to go without her?"

"Are you telling me you've never wanted to go to Belgium? That you weren't just as excited about doing a chocolate tour as Stella was?"

"Honestly? I'm not sure that I am. I think I always knew it was something we'd never do together. I mean, come on...once she got that diagnosis, all future plans were called off. She declined so fast..."

"Once you found out. I remember. But she'd been declining beforehand, too. It was in the little things that took us all longer to accept."

They were quiet for a little bit.

Mara remembered those early days. It started with tiny actions, like waiting for hours for the tea kettle to boil, or cups and plates in the fridge while leaving milk and sour cream in cupboards. Then she started missing appointments and getting lost while running simple errands...like walking down to the grocery store but ending up at the dog park across town.

Everyone gets forgetful. Everyone loses track of time. Everyone gets to the point where they've got so much on the go that they get overwhelmed easily, but when too many things happen so close together...those things become hard to ignore.

"I don't get how she managed to keep it all secret. I mean...it should have come out at some point, don't you think?"

She's not just talking about the trip.

"Maybe she did?" Amy says, not following her train of thought. "Did she ever mention the trip, but you thought she'd forgotten you'd already canceled it?"

Mara has to think about that. Had she? Sure, Stella liked to talk about all the trips she'd done when she was younger. Stella had spent a year working hard after high school and then took what she'd saved to backpack through Europe, something that was popular at the time. When she came back home, instead of going to college, she ended up raising Mara.

Mara used to wonder if she ever regretted that choice.

Even when she was lost in the memories, Stella never once complained about how her life turned out.

She used to take Mara's hands and tell her about the baby she'd raised, at how excited she was to be a mother, how she knew that was the one thing she could do and do it well.

Stella was an amazing mother.

"She probably did. She talked a lot about all the trips she took. She'd go through her photo albums all the time, telling me stories about each and every picture. But Belgium, she never talked much about it, not even at the end."

"Maybe that has to do with what was in the letter? About your father? Maybe the memories of Belgium weren't ones she wanted to remember."

"Then why go back? Why has this trip been on her bucket list for years? That's what I can't wrap my head around."

She could have kept quiet. Heck, she could have just wished Mara a happy birthday, sent her to Belgium, and never said a word about her father. So why didn't she?

As far as Mara was concerned, her father died a long, long time ago. Stella could have kept that lie going, never breathing a word about the truth, and Mara would never have been the wiser.

"How do you feel about that?"

"Finding out about my father?" She clarifies. "I really don't know. I mean, according to Mom's letter, he knew about me. Knows about me. But he's never reached out." She pauses as her massager works on one particularly tight spot on her hip. "How would you feel?"

"Angry as hell, Mara. That's how I'd feel," Amy says. "I'd want to go there and tell him off to his face, show him what he's missed by not being part of my life, then walk away, knowing this time it was my choice, not his."

Mara thinks about that for a while. When their massage is over, they head out to the pools. This is probably one of Mara's favorite things to do every time they come. There are three waterfall pools as well as a mineral pool to soak in. If the massage wasn't enough to relax her, the pools should be.

"I never knew what I was missing, Amy," Mara says, ready to talk about it now that they were soaking in a pool. "I still don't. He's only a name, a concept, someone Mom has been angry with her whole life, I guess, but that anger hasn't affected me at all. Mom was enough, you know? She made sure I had family in my life, that I've always been surrounded by people who loved me, who called me their own…even if they weren't blood."

Amy reaches out her hand and grasps tightly onto Mara. "We are your family. Don't you ever forget that. Us, Gus and Lily, your traveling girlfriends, are all the family you need. You're not alone, love, because you've got all of us."

Mara reaches out and gives Amy a long hug. "I know," she whispers.

With only an hour until their reserved tea time in the Rundle Lounge, they make their way out of the pools and into the changing rooms.

The Rundle Lounge, on the best of days, reminds Mara of a smokey bar setting with dark, subdued colors and fixtures so that the view is what stands out more than anything. And the view is amazing. With large bay windows that overlook the back patio area and mountain range, no one is paying any attention to the interior decor.

Banff is gorgeous, no matter what season it is.

As a Canadian, Mara knows how lucky she is to live here, surrounded by all this beauty.

Amy orders Goddess Oolong tea, her usual, while Mara decides to try something a little different and goes with the Ontario Icewine tea. Rather than talk, all they do is stare out at the view in front of them.

The back patio is covered with a light dusting of snow, and Adirondack chairs surround the fire pits. Off to the side is a pathway lined with lights and festive wreaths that lead to a large insulated globe where a group is gathered inside.

"Have I ever asked you where the name Tinsel Travelers came from?" Amy asks.

A grin grows across Mara's face. "Well, it wasn't from me, that's for sure. I think it was on our second Christmas Market trip in Germany that someone brought up the idea of having a group name, and getting bags and luggage tags made. They wanted a Christmas theme, and tinsel seemed appropriate considering so many of them also have grey hair."

"I love it, to be honest. It's quirky, too." Amy yawns. "That massage was exactly what I needed. After tea, we'll go back for our facials, another dip in the pool, and then I thought we could go down to the Thirsty Reindeer for a cup of their spirited hot cocoa before we head into town for dinner. There's a cute farm-to-table restaurant that recently opened. I remember you once said you wanted to try it, and I hear they have the most amazing desserts. I promise to have you home at a decent time so you can finish any last-minute packing."

"You're spoiling me too much," Mara says. "How about dinner is my treat?"

"Shush. This whole day is my birthday gift to you. Even dinner. Just enjoy it, okay?"

Their food tier arrives with the daintiest of sandwiches and desserts. Both women marvel at the display and then pick their favorites.

"What time do you leave tomorrow?" Amy asks.

"Not till later in the day. It's an overnight flight."

"Do you have everything you'll need? Do you need a ride to the airport? Should we stop at the store for some snacks on the plane?"

Mara shakes her head. "Nenita already offered, but thank you. And, it's premium economy all the way for this girl," she says with a grin. "There will be snacks and drinks, plus meals. All I probably need is chocolate, but…"

"Why bring our crappy chocolate when you're about to have the good stuff, right? Bring me back some, will you? I mean…if you have room in your luggage, that is. Are you checking a bag or doing carry-ons only?"

"You know me better than that. I am my mother's daughter, after all. Carry-on for ease and speed. Do you recall me telling you about that first trip to Europe where I took a large suitcase and the wheels broke off from having to lug that thing everywhere? Up and down the stairs in the train stations, over cobbled streets, and even lugging that thing up the stairs in some of our hotels because there was no elevator. Mom warned me on that trip, but I didn't listen… I learned my lesson, for sure."

"Sometimes, mother does know best. I expect you to post lots of photos for us to see as you travel," Amy says.

"I will...but remember, there's an eight-hour time difference, so I won't be posting until you're probably asleep."

"As long as you post them."

Mara sips at her tea, enjoying the slight scent of berry.

"Make me a promise, okay?" Amy asks. "That you will celebrate your mom while you're there. Regardless of this huge secret and the fact you could be meeting your father...remember how much your mother loved you. You're allowed to be mad, upset, disappointed...to feel all the things, but don't forget that, please?"

Mara still isn't sure how she feels. Disappointed, for sure. Angry...not yet. Confused and overwhelmed are the primary emotions that won't seem to let go.

"I don't even know if I'm going to meet the man. Unless Lucy knows more than she's ever let on, which I doubt, what did Mom expect? She told me about him because I'll be in Belgium, but it's a freakin country. Did she think I'd run into him, and we'd instantly recognize each other? I mean...it doesn't make sense, Amy, right?"

Mara wasn't lying when she said she didn't know what she was missing. Her mother was always enough for her, and she never missed not having someone to call Dad in her life.

Maybe she needs to go on this trip and do exactly what Stella asked - to make memories. Forget the big secret that her father is from Belgium. Forget all those hidden expectations and unanswered questions. This is just another ordinary Christmas Market tour with her Tinsel Travelers group, and she's going to enjoy every single moment of it.

Chapter Eight

Lucy is there to meet her as soon as she walks through the Duty-Free shop after going through security at the Calgary International Airport.

"You're finally here," she says, giving Mara a long hug. "My flight arrived early."

"Why didn't you tell me, I would have come sooner." Living in Seattle, it's surprising there wasn't a direct flight to Amsterdam for her.

Lucy waves the comment away. "I didn't want to rush you. Besides, I've been busy chatting with Kat, trying to get more details about our trip. She's being really dodgy, and it's starting to annoy me."

Mara laughs, not surprised at this. Lucy likes to be in the know, to have as much control over situations as she can, and is definitely not a loosey-goosey type of person, unlike Mara, who is fine with letting someone else plan things and take care of all the details.

"Let's just go with the flow, okay? Since this is so last minute for the both of us, why don't we just let the others take over since they've been planning things from day one?"

"I am not a *go-with-the-flow* type of person, Mara Pearce. You know this." Lucy's frown tightens for a split second before relaxing. She doesn't quite make a smile, but give her time, and she'll come around to the idea of not being in charge.

"Now that the shock has worn off, I'm kind of excited. I'll admit, I was feeling a little FOMO at not going."

"FOMO?"

"Fear of missing out, come on, Lucy, you've heard that saying before."

Lucy waves away her comment. "Listen, this woman is both a little tired and a whole lot of out of sorts. Be gentle with me, okay?"

"Out of sorts? What's going on?" Mara takes a really good look at her friend as they head toward a restaurant and catches the dark circles beneath her eyes. At sixty-five years young, Lucy is not someone Mara would ever suggest as old. She may be the oldest of their group, but she rarely ever showed it.

"Oh, don't you worry about me," Lucy says. "I'll adjust to the idea of this trip, I just wasn't expecting it, that's all."

"Well...think of it this way. You were expecting to be away from home while I went on this trip, so the only thing that's really changed is the location, right?"

Lucy's smile is forced as they store their luggage behind their table. "Right. I need to adjust my mindset. Easy peasy." The sarcasm is clear and sends a direct message. One that Mara decides to ignore.

"How about we both start over? We're doing this trip for Mom, right? What was her favorite thing to do at airports?"

"Your mother loved to people watch. It didn't matter where we were - at an airport or sitting at an outdoor cafe sipping coffee."

"Stella also believed that arriving early for a flight was a necessary part of a trip, in fact, it signified the beginning of every vacation and should be enjoyed thoroughly." If there was one thing her mother knew how to do, it was to embrace every single moment of life. It's something Mara has always tried to do as well.

"Your mother would also want us to order wine and food and then go through our itinerary to make sure we all knew what was going on. That's kind of hard to do, considering we have no idea."

"Well, we do know a little bit. You got that email from Kat about our first day in Amsterdam, right?"

Lucy tilts her head, and Mara knows instantly she has no idea what she's talking about.

"Check your email. I swear I saw you on there. She's got everyone's flight info on that list, too."

While Lucy checks her phone, a server arrives, and they order two glasses of rose and some appetizers to share.

"You realize we're all sitting at an airport right now, waiting on our flights? Well...some of the others will just be arriving at the airport, but still," Lucy says as she continues to read the email, "this time tomorrow, we'll all be in Amsterdam."

Mara hears the forced upbeatness behind Lucy's tone. At least she's trying.

"Did you see what she has planned? I mean...it sounds like a lot of fun, right? Have you ever been to the city? Is it as gorgeous as the photos you see online?"

A soft smile appears as Lucy tucks a sliver of hair beneath her ear. "I've been, and yes, it's quite lovely. Unlike any other city, actually. Looks like she has us going on a chocolate walk, eating Dutch pancakes, tasting apple pie, going on a canal cruise, and then..."

"Wait, there's chocolate in Amsterdam?" Mara's a little surprised at that. Honestly she hadn't thought of it until now.

"Silly question. Of course, there is. Not as much as in Belgium, but apparently, Kat found enough of them to do an official chocolate walk. Did you see that part about the dining-in-the-dark experience, too? What is that about?"

While Mara waits, Lucy does a search for the event. "Oh, that's kind of cool. Your mother would have loved this. Its a chocolate dessert course enjoyed while in a completely black room. There is no light whatsoever, and in fact, we'll be served by people who are blind." She looks up with a thoughtful look. "That sounds interesting."

It does, and Stella would have loved every second of it. "So, I guess wearing white is out of the question."

"Or wear a bib," Lucy teases. "Oh my goodness, do you remember that time in Florida when your mother pulled out a bib at that pasta place? She said she didn't want to get her shirt dirty."

"Mom always kept a bib in her purse. She didn't care what she looked like with it on. I think her favorite was that one you got her from Maine. With that huge lobster on it?"

They both chuckle at the memory.

"Making your mother laugh was always a fun pastime for me. It was infectious."

They're both quiet for a moment as if privately remembering Stella.

"I miss her. I've missed who she was for a long time, but now, I miss...her. Her presence. Her smile. And the way she could laugh at anything. I'm also...really confused, Lucy." Mara admits.

Lucy nods. "I don't doubt you are."

"I read her other letter. She says you have more?"

Lucy nods. She looks like she's about to say something, but Mara cuts her off.

"Don't worry, I'm not going to ask for them. I'm not ready for any more of Mom's surprises. I assume you know the part about my father being from Belgium?" She sees the confirmation in Lucy's eyes. "Yeah, well, finding out my father isn't dead...that's enough for now. I don't even know how to process that. I mean... how can he be alive and not in my life? Mom said something about him choosing his family over us, but what does that mean? Why cut someone out of your life so completely that they don't even know you exist?"

Lucy looks like she has something to say, but she instead takes her wine glass and twirls it around before taking a sip.

"Did she ever tell you about him?" Mara asks, insanely curious about the answer.

It takes a while, but Lucy finally nods. "She did. There's...a lot to the story, and I know some, but..." The sigh Lucy gives is full of disappointment and something else...Mara can't quite pinpoint what the other emotion is.

"I don't even know how to feel about all of this, to be honest. I wish...I wish she'd never said anything. Waiting until she is dead to reveal a truth bomb like that isn't fair. If I didn't need to know while she was alive, why do I need to know all of this now that she's dead?"

"She had her reasons," Lucy says. "I never agreed with her, but ultimately—"

"This isn't your story to tell, is it?" Mara finishes for her.

Lucy gives a slight shrug as if to say, *I guess*, and while it feels like the woman knows more, Mara isn't going to prod. Not just yet.

"Your mother and I have known each other a long time, Mara. And there's a lot about my past you don't know." Lucy drains her glass and looks around for a server. "One more can't hurt, right? I know they say not to drink a lot before a flight or even on a flight, but damn, I think I need it." She orders another glass while Mara asks for a refill of her water.

"Listen, Mara. I didn't want to come on this trip for a reason, but here I am, whether I like it or not, and to be honest, I think your mother made sure she was gone before the trip just for this very reason. It wouldn't surprise me." Lucy plays with the glass in her hand. "I always told your mother she would regret some of the decisions she'd made, but she made me promise to keep her secrets, and because I love her and you, I've done just that."

"Mom always said people will always make decisions they regret later, but sometimes you have to live in that regret and accept what comes rather than wish you could change things."

Lucy leans back in her chair. "Your mother wasn't always right,

A Belgium Chocolate Christmas

you realize that I hope." She heaves a long sigh. "So, Kat doesn't mention anything past our days in Amsterdam, right?"

Mara shakes her head. "We play tourist and then head to Brussels, I'm assuming. You know, I don't think I've ever asked. Have you been to Belgium before? If we have a home base in Brussels, is it easy to get around via the trains to the other towns?"

A look full of too many emotions for Mara to even attempt a guess at, crosses Lucy's face.

"Actually, it'll be like returning home," she says wistfully.

Mara sits back hard in her seat. "I'm sorry?" She thought Lucy grew up in the United States. She lives in Seattle, and for some reason, Mara always assumed that was home to her.

"Surprise, surprise, right? It's been years since I've been back. I'm honestly not sure how I feel about it. I left for a reason, never thinking I'd ever return. Truth be told, I never really wanted to."

"So that's why you're off-kilter? Because you're returning home?" This news surprises her. She feels like she should know Lucy better and yet, she obviously doesn't. "You don't have to if it's going to be too hard for you."

"I'm not someone who tends to run from things just because it might hurt. You know that."

"Yeah, but still." For some reason, Mara feels guilty that Lucy is coming like it's her fault for some reason, which is ridiculous. "I had no idea, Lucy. I'm assuming Mom did though, right?"

There's a look on Lucy's face that answers her question.

"Will we be close to your family? I mean...please go see them, if we are. I know the others will understand."

Lucy actually snorts as a response.

"Or not," Mara says.

"It'll be fine. I might take a day or two to myself while you all explore, but...this trip isn't about me, okay? I need you to remember that. It's about making memories and maybe getting to understand your mother a little better. Plus...all the chocolate. I mean...how can we be in Belgium and not eat all the chocolate?"

Lucy glances at her watch. "We'll be boarding soon. Did you need to grab anything from the stores here?"

"Maybe just a coffee to take on the plane," Mara says. "I also want to get some gift cards for the flight attendants, as a thanks, you know, keep on Mom's tradition and all."

Stella used to gift the attendants with little gifts, a small way to say thank you for putting up with us all. She said being a flight attendant was a thankless job, especially having to put up with privileged and entitled travelers.

"Your mom was always good like that. Tell you what, I'll grab a box of chocolates from the Rocky Mountain shop over there, and you get those coffee cards."

This was Mom's trip, after all, so why not start it off right? Mara drains the last of her wine and softly whispers, *I miss you, Mom*, as she gathers her things.

Chapter Nine

Mara and Lucy were the last to arrive after having to land in London for a medical emergency. They thought for sure all the others would have left to check into their hotel, but they were all there, waiting at the gate.

It's a swarm of hugs before they walk toward the exit.

"Now, I know we generally get a transfer to our hotels, but the trains here are so easy, and our hotel is so close, that I figured we could try something new," Kat says as she leads them toward the escalators leading to the train platform. "Lucy and Mara, we already bought your tickets, but make sure you keep them on you. Apparently, we need them to exit the station later or pay a fine."

"I can't believe we're here." Donna pulls her luggage behind her. "I also can't believe the two of you only brought carry-ons. I tried, but between the extra jacket I brought, plus the need for both shoes and boots, it wasn't possible."

Mara looks at everyone's luggage. "Seriously, did Stella not teach you anything? You know she'd be reaming you all out about now." She gives them all a saucy wink. "It's a good thing I'm nothing like my mother."

"I couldn't do it either," Sandra admits. "Last time, I had to ship stuff home because I had no room, and do you know how expensive that is? At least this way, I know I'll have room between the larger suitcase and my backpack."

They cram onto the train, everyone finding seats and trying hard to keep their luggage out of the way. Kat ends up next to Mara.

"How was the flight? Did you get any sleep? I tried, but there was a crying baby close by, and not even earplugs could muffle that sound."

"I've never been able to sleep on the plane, crazy, right?"

"I remember. I also remember you tend to get a little grumpy during our first day because of it." Kat nudges her in the side as she pulls out a chocolate bar from her purse. "Here, a little pick-me-up."

Mara's smile comes easy seeing the chocolate. She slowly unwraps it and breaks off a piece. "True, but I'm not the only one, either. Looks like you're going to keep us busy, though, which is good. Hopefully, I'll crash tonight."

"Well, it's either crash or be wide awake. That's usually my problem. I'm at that insomnia and hot flash stage of my life, and let me tell you, it sucks."

It's raining by the time they exit Amsterdam Central Station.

"Rain in November? Why can't it be snowing? And where are all the market stalls? I thought we'd see all things Christmas?" Jo-Jo complains as everyone fiddles with either their raincoats or umbrellas.

"Aren't you glad you listened to me about the raincoats? Plus, we're too early for the markets here," Kat says. "They start till for another few weeks, trust me, I looked. Remember, we came here because it was the cheapest flight, not because of the markets."

"Can't we just Uber to where we're headed?" Donna asks as she shrugs on her raincoat and pulls up her hood.

"There are no vehicles within the core, and we're only a few blocks away. It's not like you're going to melt," Kat shoots the woman a saucy grin before she pushes open the doors and steps outside.

Mara keeps quiet, but she agrees with Donna. On any other trip, they had private transfers from the airport to their hotel.

It's a grey and dismal day in Amsterdam, but that doesn't seem to keep the people away. The sidewalks are crowded, even with the weather, and it's hard for their group to steer through them while also attempting to avoid the puddles.

"Are you sure it's close?" Mara grumbles as they wait at a crosswalk.

"Keep an eye on the bicycles," Lucy warns. "There are more bicycles in Amsterdam than there are vehicles, and it's not their fault we're not paying attention."

"Come on, we're almost there." Kat stares at the map on her phone. "Sorry guys, guess we should have done the transfers."

They head down a street, turn left, and then an immediate right until they are in a small alleyway that leads to another busy street, but this one has construction barriers everywhere and wood planks instead of sidewalks.

"I vote we always use transfers from now on," Jo-Jo grumbles. "Please tell me there's one in Brussels, right?"

"Stephanie already took care of that," Kat confirms.

Once they reach their hotel, all Mara wants to do is jump in a warm shower and then drink a large glass of coffee. Then maybe have a nap if there's enough time.

"No napping," Lucy reminds her as they settle into their room. "I promise we'll go to sleep early tonight, but we have to stay awake until then."

"That's about the only thing about traveling overseas I hate," Mara says. "The first day is such a waste, because you hardly remember it from being so sleep deprived, and then once you do go to bed, either you sleep like a log, or you wide awake for the rest of the night."

"Hurry up with that shower," Lucy says. "I need to get some caffeine in you to take the grumpiness away."

Mara grabs her toiletries and heads to the bathroom. The second she opens the door and looks down, she closes it again.

"Um, Lucy, there's bugs in our bathroom." She gives a small shudder as she backs away. Opening the door turned on the automatic lights. The only thing she saw was a scurry of creepy crawlies heading toward the drain in the middle of the floor.

Mara hates bugs.

"There's what?" Lucy opens the bathroom door and then quickly closes it. "Nope. Grab your stuff. We are not staying in this room."

While they repack, Lucy grabs the phone and calls down to the front desk. In her no-nonsense way, she informs them they need a new room on account of the bugs in their current one. By the time they exit the elevator, a hotel worker is waiting for them.

"I'm sorry about the bugs. Please, follow me; we have a new room for you." They cross the main lobby, and into a different area of the hotel. "This section has been recently renovated, and we've upgraded you. You'll be on the same floor as the others in your party."

Their new room is not only larger, but nicer too.

"Well, this is better," Lucy says after investigating the bathroom for bugs. "Mara, check the bed too, will you? Just to make sure," she says before the staff member leaves.

Mara lifts up the corner covers and checks the seams of the mattress for any evidence of bed bugs. They do this on every single trip, and so far, they've never had an issue.

"We should have been on the same floor as the others in the first place." Lucy bares no bones about being disgruntled.

"Yes, I'm sorry about that. It looks like you were a late booking, but we recently had a cancellation. Otherwise, the hotel is fully booked."

Mara waits till they're alone. "Lucy, you could have been nicer."

"Being nice all the time doesn't always get you anywhere," Lucy says. "Sometimes the direct approach is the only approach. Especially here. You can be the nice Canadian all you want, Mara, but if it were left to you, we'd be sleeping in that bug-infested room."

"Ouch. Now, who's grumpy? Thank you for saying something, I'll hurry with my shower so we can meet up with everyone. How much time do we have left?" Kat had given everyone a time to meet down in the reception area.

"You've got thirty minutes, give or take. I think I'll head downstairs and grab a coffee. Text me when you come down, okay?"

It takes one quick shower, two glasses of coffee, and sharing a bar of chocolate with the others down in the coffee room before everyone is ready to head out.

"So, what's the plan for today?" Mara asks Kat as they walk down the street.

Turning so she's walking backward and facing everyone, Kat has the widest smile on her face. "We're going to walk till we drop if that's okay with you all. I've got a few bakeries and chocolate shops on my list, and while we walk, we'll stop for a freshly made stroopwafel, which was one of the things you all said you wanted to try."

As a group, they always put in requests for restaurants they want to visit, or special foods that were all the hype on social media. Mara hadn't participated in those discussions for this trip.

"Walking and eating sounds perfect. At least the rain has stopped." Sandra says.

"There's also a flower market to explore. Stephanie booked us on a canal cruise, and then before we're done, we'll eat the best apple pie around, and not all in that order, either. The goal is to walk our ten thousand-plus steps and then crash for the night. Tomorrow is the big day of sightseeing."

"When are we going to do that dining in the dark chocolate thing you told us about?" Mara asks, now walking beside Kat.

"Tomorrow." There's a level of excitement in Kat's voice that is equally matched to the grip on her arm as they stop in front of a cute little shop.

"Coco & Sebas," Kat says. "Look at those chocolates, girls. We have to try one, don't you think? I'm told we have to try the hot chocolate here. It's one of the best in the city."

"Sounds delicious," Mara says as they enter the store and breathe in the sweet aroma of chocolate.

By the back counter, they see an open faucet with chocolate running into a drain. They all order hot cocoa and watch as their cups are filled from that chocolate faucet. Jo-Jo even records it with her phone.

"Mara," Kat turns to her with a serious look on her face. "Your mother had a talk with me about this trip. She was very precise in her wants and locations to visit and explore. She was also very specific about the chocolate. According to her wishes, we must buy at least one piece of chocolate from every store we visit," Kat explains as they both peer into the display cases.

"She had a talk with you? When?" Stella's lucidity was almost gone for most of the year, and when she was in a chatty mood, Mara could never truly follow the conversation.

"A few years ago." Kat gives her a look, a look that is full of sympathy and empathy all rolled in one. "She didn't know when we'd get to Belgium, but when we did, she had a list of suggestions. Well, I guess they weren't suggestions but more like instructions." She lifts a shoulder in a shrug. "You know how your Mom is, was…"

Lucy laughs, an obvious attempt to break the awkwardness. "That's so like Stella. I'm not surprised with her request for the chocolate, either. You couldn't drag her out of a chocolate shop without her buying something first."

Mara gives Kat a slight nod, letting her know she understands and is okay with the slip and looks around the shop. They're supposed to try at least one piece? That might be an issue because so many of them look amazing. From the milk chocolate to the dark, to the caramel and ruby...how is she supposed to pick just one?

In the end, Mara buys a box of assorted chocolates with every flavor from the store and shares it with the everyone.

"How about we take turns buying these?" Donna suggests as she takes a caramel treat. "We'll go from youngest to oldest since Mara already bought the first round."

"That's a great idea," Lucy says.

Between the hot cocoa, which is nothing like what Mara makes at home, to the melt-in-your-mouth chocolate, she wasn't feeling as grumpy as before, but then how could she remain grumpy in a city like this?

Amsterdam is a magical city, and despite having never placed it on her #mustvisit list, Mara vows to return one day for a much longer stay. Between the winding streets, the flower boxes along the bridges, and the picture-worthy canal shots - even in the rain...the city has placed a foothold in Mara's wandering heart.

Chapter Ten

They walk through the Red-light district to find one of the most distinct chocolate shops she's ever seen. Ganache is housed in a picture-perfect little storefront that backs onto an old church, one of the oldest in the city center. Inside, the chocolate is everywhere, from amazing basket designs to the tulips associated with the city. There were chocolate-covered coffee beans and malt balls, and they all walked out of there with boxes full of delicious treats.

"I think that's my favorite shop we've ever been in," Lucy says, "and traveling with Stella, I've been in several chocolate stores."

They slowly make their way up the streets toward the floating flower market, stopping at several pastry shops, marveling over the huge chocolate-dipped strawberries and waffles they see in all the window displays until they find the van Wonderen Stroopwafels store. The smell greets them halfway down the block, and they didn't need the map on Kat's phone, the line out the door is enough of an indicator that they found the right place.

"You might need to hold me back," Lucy says as she peers around the crowds to see inside the shop. "I've been dreaming about eating these again for years. Having one freshly made is the only real way to eat a stroopwafel. Sure, the ones you buy in the shop and eat with your coffee are fine, but trust me when I say, you'll never taste anything better than a fresh one made to order."

Lucy isn't kidding. As Mara nibbles on hers while they walk, she has to stop herself from moaning with delight at the delicate balance between thin cookie and caramel.

"Wait, you've been here before?" Jo-Jo finally clues into what Lucy said earlier. It's taken everything for Mara not to say anything.

Lucy nods. "I guess it's only fair I tell you all, too." She glances over at Mara, who takes a step back.

"Don't look at me," Mara says as she feels everyone's gaze on her. "I only just found out, too."

"I was born in Belgium and grew up in a small town there. I went to the States for a one-year course, fell in love and the rest is history, I guess you can say. It's been a long time since I've been back." She stares down at the cookie in her hand. "Actually, I never wanted to come back here, if I'm being honest, and no, I'm not going to expand on that. This trip isn't a homecoming for me, in case you're wondering. I'm here for Mara and Stella and because it's our bi-annual Market trip." She harrumphs as only Lucy does before she turns and continues walking down the street. "Where to next, Kat?" She asks in a no-nonsense tone.

"Wait, you didn't answer my question," Jo-Jo says as she rushes to catch up to Lucy's rushed walking. "Why didn't you ever mention you've been here before? You could have helped with the planning. Out of all of us, you know the place the best."

Lucy shakes her head. "I was here as a teenager. The city I knew and the one we're visiting now are different. I mean, they didn't have Ganache back then. And besides, when I came here, it was with friends. We'd take the train and crash on someone's couch...you know how teenagers are. I was...well, I was a wild child, I guess you can say."

Mara's laugh is a little forced, but she's not the only one trying to lighten the mood.

"I'm trying to picture you as a wild child," Sandra says, pushing her bangs out of her eyes with her one free hand. "I mean, when it comes to having fun, you're always right in the thick of things, but...well, I guess it's really not hard to picture after all."

Mara has no problem imagining that. Stella always said Lucy was her soul sister, and while on their trips, or even whenever Lucy came to visit, those two women always ended up having fun together.

"I remember Mom telling me once about a friend she'd made during her year in Europe. She said losing touch with someone who knew her inside and out had been hard for her." Mara pauses and looks at Lucy. "You know, it's too bad you and Mom didn't know each other when she was here," Mara says.

"Why do you say that?" Lucy's voice is soft and hesitant.

"I don't know...I guess I'm looking at things differently now. You two were so close...it's too bad you didn't meet sooner, you know?"

Lucy moves through the group and grabs her arm, giving it a slight squeeze. "Your mother will always be the absolute bestest friend I could ever have wished for. We were sisters, Mara. There's an ache in my heart now I'm not sure will ever go away," she confesses, looking off into the distance.

"Come on," Kat says, interjecting, "just around the corner is the flower market. Lucy, I'm sure they had this when you were a teen, right? Girls, we should all buy some bulbs to plant back home. And grab yourself a vase while you're at it. Then, every spring, when the tulips bloom, we can all have a piece of the Netherlands in our home."

The flower market spans the length of one block and is full of vendors selling fresh flowers, flower bulbs, Christmas ornaments, and even clunky wooden tulips.

Mara takes her time, mainly because she wants to see everything and take it all in but also because she is starting to lag and is more than ready to head back to their hotel. They've already hit their ten thousand steps for the day. She's sure of it.

She smothers a yawn, hoping no one notices.

"Do we get an ornament for Amsterdam, or do we wait till we're at an actual market?" Mara asks Lucy.

Ornaments are a huge part of their tradition as a group. In every market they visit, they buy one ornament each. Some of the women like to have multiple trees in their homes - one for the family and one showcasing their market ornaments. Stella and she only ever had one tree, and it was full of both the homemade ones she'd made as a child in school and the ones they bought at the markets.

"I think you should get this one," Lucy says as she hands her a house in the blue Delft style. "I'll get one too. Oh, you know what...you should do one of those Market baskets in the store. You could include one of these in there, along with some chocolate and other things we'll find."

Mara nods. She'd totally forgotten about those baskets she usually makes up at Christmas. Every year following a market trip, she'd make up a few baskets to give away to customers in the store. Gus would use it as a promotion for the holidays, and they were always popular. Some would be ornaments and household items, and some would be just chocolate baskets.

"I should have brought a bigger suitcase," Mara says, twerking her lips as she decides on an ornament to purchase. She grabs a few, one in the shape of a tulip, one in the shape of a clog, and one that looks like the houses along the canals.

Mara tries to smother another yawn and notices that one by one, everyone in their group copies her.

"Okay, ladies. Let's keep moving. We can head down to our canal cruise, which is by the train station, which means, when we're done, it's a short walk back to the hotel, okay?"

The rain starts to fall again, and their walk down to the train station is a quiet one.

"I'm so ready for bed," Mara says just as she yawns again.

"What about that famous apple pie?" Donna asks.

"Right. Cruise, pie, then bed."

"Tell me about this apple pie," Mara says. "I need you to sell it to me."

"Kat, are you talking about the Papeneiland Cafe?" Lucy asks. "If so, you'll all want to stay awake for that, I promise."

"Oh, you know about it, Lucy?" Kat asks.

"Know about it? It's only one of the famous brown bars here in Amsterdam."

"A what?"

Lucy smiles. "Weird name, right? It's a whole culture in Amsterdam. They're called Brown Bars because of their rich coziness with dark walls and furniture. My friends and I would sit upstairs by the windows for hours. The apple pie is unlike anything you've had here, trust me."

Once again, Lucy is right. The cafe is only a few blocks from their hotel and from where their canal cruise ended.

It's dark inside, but once her eyes adjust, Mara has an instant connection with the place. Worn brown paneling covered the walls, along with framed art and the iconic blue Delft plates. There isn't much seating available, so they climb the narrow stairs to find a free table.

"That's where I'd sit with friends," Lucy points toward a loud group clustered around a table. "We'd drink our beer, eat off of everyone's plates, and talk about...well, about everything, I guess." She smiles wistfully, lost in her memories.

"So, what do you think?" Lucy asks.

Mara nods. "This place is amazing. I don't know about everyone else though, but I need to redo the canal cruise...I swear I nodded off for most of it."

"I think we all did," Kat says. "Maybe doing that ride on our first night wasn't the smartest idea, but it was the only time in our schedule. Sorry, guys."

"It was nice to get out of the rain for a bit, at least. We should come back sometime and explore the streets more. Maybe we could come during the tulip season? Plus, who knew there'd be so many cheese shops."

"There's more than I remember, for sure," Lucy says.

"I'm still amazed that you're from here," Mara says in a low voice to Lucy, who sits beside her. "Not here. Belgium."

"There's a huge difference between the two countries. But I know what you mean. I did live a full life before we all met on that first trip of ours." Lucy says.

"I know...to be honest, I never thought about it. I mean...it feels like you've always been in my life, you know? One minute, we met on a trip to Paris, and the next thing I knew, you were at the house having dinner with us. I think you were Mom's closest friend, too."

"I've always loved your mother," Lucy looks away, her lips lightly trembling. "We talked about moving in together once, you know? When you eventually moved out to live your own life, before..."

"Before dementia set in."

As soon as she suspected something was wrong with her mom, all of Mara's life plans were placed on hold. She'd wanted to become a pastry chef, train in Paris, then come back and open up a patisserie in the mountains. Now, all she does is read cookbooks, watch videos online, and dabble at trying new recipes.

"We all had so many plans. Didn't you and Mom talk about doing one of those yearly cruises around the world?"

Lucy laughs. "Oh my goodness, I forgot all about that. It was your mom's idea, you know? Said it would be cheaper to live on a cruise ship for a year than to pay rent, buy food, and plan yearly vacation trips. Now, wouldn't that have been a hoot?" She lets out a long sigh. "I thought your mom and I would grow old together, be those two best friends who yelled at each other from different chairs because we couldn't hear anymore."

"I can picture that."

"So could I. Letting go of that dream was hard. I miss her," Lucy pats Mara's hand. "Your mother was one of a kind, that's for sure.

Their apple pies arrive with a large dollop of cream, and silence reigns around the table as they all inhale the delicious treat.

"That is nothing like the apple pie I make at home," Mara says after licking her fork.

"Kat, when researching this place, did you read about it's history?" Lucy asks. "Downstairs, there should still be a green gate. This place was part of a larger group with hidden tunnels that, during the Reformation, allowed Catholics to walk to church without getting caught. Amsterdam was full of hidden or secret churches back then."

"Can we go into the tunnel?" Donna asks.

Lucy shrugs. "I doubt it. We couldn't back then, and it's probably not safe anymore. But these tunnels are all over. I'll show you the door, though, when we leave."

"Is everyone ready?" Kat asks. "We have a day of sightseeing tomorrow, but I could use a nice soak in the hotel's hot tub before heading to bed. What do you say?"

Mara has no words, just a light moan at how amazing that sounds.

"Lead the way."

Chapter Eleven

Zaanse Schans. It sounds like a song and swear word all mixed in one, but it's a quaint, historic town with working windmills and adorable tourist shops.

What Mara loves the most about this town, however, is the smell. The tour guide from the bus warned that it would have a distinct aroma, and Mara has to agree.

With chocolate factories being close by, the moment you step out of the bus, you're hit with a warm, delicious hint of a whiff carried along the breeze…a whiff of chocolate, of sweetness…if Mara could bottle it, she would.

"Are you smelling that too? I thought the guide was kidding," Lucy says, pulling her to the side. "Take a look at this place, Mara, it's adorable."

Adorable doesn't cut it. It's quaint and picturesque and everything Mara expected from a windmill town. It's a small village on the banks of the Zaan River, and not only is it a working town, but people still live close by if the view as they cross the curved wooden bridge is any indication. Off in the distance is a town she'd love to visit if there's time.

Although from the itinerary their tour guide gave them, she has a feeling that's not an option.

"Is there a way we can skip the rest of the tour and stay here instead? Maybe grab a taxi back afterward? I don't think they're giving us enough time here," Jo-Jo pushes herself in between Mara and Lucy and holds up a pamphlet she'd grabbed from a wooden wall full of information. "I mean, there's a chocolate museum behind us where we could have made our own chocolate. Come on - chocolate or cheese, like there's really a choice, right?"

Mara looks around for Kat. "Did you mention it to Kat?"

"God no," Jo-Jo whispers in a dramatic tone. "That woman hates alterations made to her schedules. You know that."

"Besides, did you listen to the itinerary for today? I can't believe I'm about to say this, but there is such a thing as too much chocolate, and I'm looking forward to seaside villages and cheese." Mara ducks as Lucy swings and slaps her shoulder.

"I don't ever want to hear you say something like that again, do you hear me? Too much chocolate? Who are you kidding? I know all about your chocolate stashes around your apartment and in the store."

Mara's eyes are wide with innocence.

"Oh, don't even...how much chocolate do you have in that bag of yours right now?" Lucy goes and opens Mara's bag, chucking as she peers inside. "I knew it," she says as she sees the small box of chocolates from a store they'd visited yesterday.

"And your bag doesn't have any, right?" Mara's sarcasm isn't masked as she peers into Lucy's bag. "You leave my chocolate alone, you hear? I asked if you wanted me to bring you any, and you said no, that you'd find some today as we take our tour."

Kat waves at them to hurry up and join the tour.

"I can't believe people actually live here," Lucy says as they follow the group leading toward the windmills. "And those big things all still work, did you know that?"

A Belgium Chocolate Christmas

"Those big things are called windmills," Mara says with a bit of cheek. She turns to find Jo-Jo snapping away with her phone.

"These are going to look so great on social media," Jo-Jo says. "Smile, girls."

"Do you want to see the windmills, or do you want to do some shopping?" Lucy asks. "I'm sure everything here is overpriced, but..."

"Why don't you shop while I tour, and I'll meet up with you after?" Touring the windmills looks interesting, and she's not that much of a shopper, unlike Lucy.

The tour guide wasn't kidding that they weren't there for very long. After walking through one windmill, Mara realizes she only has fifteen minutes before she needs to be back on the bus, and she still hasn't checked out the shop with the hot chocolate sign out front.

Inside, she meets Lucy, who has a basket full of goodies. "Oh good, I was wondering where you were. I bought us some hot cocoa mixes and tea towels. Come on...before we head back to the bus, I found this cute display of wooden shoes I want you to see."

They power walk as best they can through the crowds until they come to a set of large wooden shoes with people getting their pictures taken. The shoes are set up in a heart pattern.

"Adorable, right?" Lucy hands her phone to a stranger and asks them to take a picture.

"That seems to be the word of the day," Mara teases.

"I honestly thought we'd have more time here." Lucy pulls out the printed itinerary Mara had given them all for the day. "Says two hours..."

"Well...technically, it's been almost two hours since we got on the bus. Maybe it includes travel time, too."

Lucy nods. "Maybe. Guess it makes sense, considering how packed this day is."

Kat found them in time to make the bus. "I can't believe you two are the last to arrive," she hisses. "Although, I shouldn't be surprised. I've got my eyes on you ladies," she warns as she sits in her seat.

Their next stop has them in Volendam, a small fishing village where they all buy some cheese, and Sandra finds a cute traditional outfit she swears she'll wear for Halloween next year. They all order hot cocoa while on a ferry boat across a large lake and share their purchases.

Mara's favorite part of the tour was visiting the Delft Pottery Museum, and that's mainly because of her mother. Stella loved Delft pottery. There's a plate, teacup, and saucer in the china cabinet back at home that her mom had treasured. She bought it during her year abroad, and today, of all days, Mara feels a connection to Stella. Her mother would have loved this place. Most things here are out of her price range, but she does manage to find a cute little tea bag holder that will be perfect for the kitchen. Stella used to marvel at the fact every plate and vase was handprinted, and after watching the demonstration of someone painting a large vase, she finally understands Stella's obsession.

Exhaustion hits on the coach ride home, and no matter how hard she tries, she can't keep her eyes open.

"Mara, wake up." She hears Lucy's voice but wants to ignore it. "Mara, everyone is getting off the bus."

That's all it takes for her eyes to pop open, and she bolts up out of her seat. "I can't believe I fell asleep," she says as she gathers all her belongings, making sure she doesn't leave anything behind. She's done that a few times in the past, but Stella was always there to grab her things for her.

"Did you grab the bag you put up in the top area?"

Mara quickly grabs it, giving Lucy a smile in thanks.

"Okay, ladies," Kat says once they're all together behind the train terminal where the bus dropped them off, "so here's what's happening. We'll head back to the hotel where you can grab a small bite to eat, or have a little nap," she looks to Mara and gives her a wink. "I have a transfer coming to pick us up at the hotel for six thirty to take us to our dessert party."

"This is the eating-in-the-dark experience, right?" Lucy asks.

Kat nods. "I have no idea how messy it will get, so I advise maybe not wearing white."

"This is going to be so much fun. Do you think I'll be able to take photos?" Jo-Jo asks.

"It's in the dark, honey, with no lights," Lucy says.

"Yeah, but my camera takes amazing night photos..." She stops from saying anything else as it clicks in. "Oh, it'll be completely in the dark. Got it."

As they head to the hotel, a few in the group splinter off to do more shopping, but all Mara wants to do is crash on her bed and have a good nap.

"Today's a day your mother would have loved, don't you think?" Lucy says as they enter their room together.

"She would have gone nuts at the Delft museum and probably spent her whole budget there." Mara eases back on the bed with a sigh. "I miss her. I felt her presence with me a lot today."

"I don't want to feel that presence with us tonight," Lucy says. "No ghosts in the dark, you hear me, Stella Pearce," she glances up toward the ceiling with a smile.

Chapter Twelve

They take the tram across the city and then go to CTaste, where their fondue-in-the-dark experience is about to occur.

They're the only ones there as they walk into the dim location.

"Are we in the right place?" Lucy stays close to the door, one hand on the handle. "This doesn't look like a restaurant at all."

Mara can't help but agree with her. There's a long bench to the left where the rest of the group sits, and to the right is a counter with a cash register. The area is narrow, and there's not much light.

"Are you sure, Kat? I mean...there's no one here." Lucy clutches her coat tight around her.

Kat heads to the counter and rings the bell. From around the corner, a man appears.

"Welcome to CTaste," he says. "My name is Victor. Is this your first time here?"

One by one, they all nod.

"Then this is going to be quite the experience," he says. "Let me take your coats, please." He holds out a hand and takes their jackets one by one, hanging them up behind a black curtain. "We have lockers for everyone to place their bags around the corner, and please don't lose your keys."

Once everyone has locked their purses, they stand in a long hallway, unprepared for what's to come. "You're all nervous, I can tell. Don't be. This will be a night to remember, I promise. One of our servers will come out and guide you into our dining area, where it is completely black."

"What do you mean by completely black?" Jo-Jo asks.

"There is zero light."

"Oh, I've heard of places like this. I've always wanted to do one of these experiences," Jo-Jo says.

"How will we be served then? How will we see what we're eating?" Lucy asks, her voice rising with each sentence she utters.

"It'll be okay, Lucy," Mara puts her arm around her friend's waist and gives it a squeeze. "Mom would love this, let's focus on that."

Lucy lets out a sigh and nods.

"Our staff are all legally blind," Victor explains. "You'll be dining with their help. When you walk in, you'll place your hand on your guide's shoulder, and he'll walk you to your table. He'll then explain everything to you."

"But..."

"We'll figure it out, Lucy. It's all part of the experience, right?" Mara says.

Lucy shrugs. "I hate not knowing all the details, you know that."

It's not that Lucy needs to be in control of every situation she's in, but rather, she needs to be prepared for what's to come.

"Hello, I'm Alex," a man wearing all black walks through a curtained doorway. "Are you ready for your fondue in the dark?" His grin is wide, and while he seems to be staring right at them, Mara notices right away he doesn't see them. "If you'll follow me?"

He waits at the curtained doorway and has Lucy place her hand on his shoulder, then has Mara place hers on Lucy's shoulder, with everyone else following suit. Mara hears Jo-Jo giggle.

"I'll walk slowly," Alex says. "You won't be able to see anything inside, but when it comes to chocolate, all your other senses will be used anyway, right?"

They shuffle along, the curtain brushing past them as they make their way into a midnight-black room. The first few moments are a huge adjustment, their eyes taking time to adjust.

"This is crazy," Donna whispers behind Mara. "I can't even see your head, Mara." Other than Donna's whispers, the only sound they hear is their feet shuffling along the floor.

Mara knew they'd be eating in the dark but wasn't prepared for just how dark the dark is. There's always a light on somewhere at home, even if it's a nightlight in the hallway.

Alex leads them to their table, his steps slow but sure. He directs them to feel for the bench and to slide along until they are next to a wall. Mara goes in first. They are instructed to use their hands to feel for the plate and silverware in front of them.

"There's also a pitcher of water," he says, as Mara's hand bumps into the jug.

"And we're supposed to pour it? Without spilling it all over ourselves?" Lucy starts laughing.

"I've got this," Mara says. She carefully grasps onto the handle with one hand, and then moves her own glass closer. She holds the edge of her glass to the jug and slowly fills it, using the tip of her finger to measure where to stop. "If everyone gives me their glass, I can fill it." She keeps her movements slow, not wanting to spill... much.

"In a few moments, I will be bringing out your fondue and trays. There will be an assortment for you to dip into the chocolate, but I'll keep what you're eating as a surprise. I will also bring you a small bowl of ice cream for you to enjoy. Let your senses guide you, I promise you won't be disappointed."

At first, it's a little unnerving sitting there in complete darkness, but it doesn't take long for Mara to adjust. In fact, it's quite nice. She has no idea if there are other diners in the room or if it's just their group. There's a hushed ambiance that is both warm and welcoming, and Mara finds herself relaxing back against her chair.

In no time, Alex returns and sets a large round tray on their table. One by one, he takes their hands and guides them to the edge of the platter and then toward the middle, where a large round bowl rests.

"This is the chocolate. It's a little warm, so be careful," he warns before he leaves.

Letting their fingers explore, the girls all discover the foods on the platter. They all call out what they feel. Strawberries, watermelon, pineapple, gummy bears, and different types of cookies.

Everything and anything that can be dipped in chocolate seems to be there.

Mara focuses on the small bowl of ice cream. Holding her bowl as close to the chocolate as possible, she spoons some into her bowl, then brings the bowl up to her lips, careful not to spill.

"This is so much fun," Mara says in between her bites of ice cream. "I need to do this back home, maybe host it at Amy's diner...can you imagine how fun this would be."

"You totally should," Jo-Jo says.

"Anyone worried about all the chocolate they've dribbled on their shirts?"

"I've probably got smears all over my face," Sandra mutters. Mara can't tell if she's enjoying herself or not.

"Well, I, for one, am glad we did this," Kat says, her voice filled with a smile. "Not only is it delicious, but it's fun and unexpected and something I would never have done otherwise."

"And I'm glad I'm doing it with all of you," Lucy says. "Stella would have loved it too, don't you think? She'd have pulled out her bib though to cover her top."

Mara snorts. "We probably should have done that ourselves," she says, her fingers searching along the tabletop for a napkin.

"It's too late for me," Lucy says. "It's a good thing it's dark outside, so no one will see the mess we've made."

The conversation dwindles as they enjoy dipping their food into the delicious, decadent dessert.

It's not until after Alex returns and takes the tray away, promising to return with coffee, that the mood around the table changes.

"Tomorrow is a travel day," Kat says. "So, we're headed to Brussels, where we'll stay for a few days and then—"

"A few days? We have five days left of this trip. Where else are we headed?" There's an edge to Lucy's voice that Mara catches. Does anyone else?

"Well, that's where Stella comes in."

If ever there is a time she wishes she could see Kat's face, it's right now.

"I guess now is as good a time as any," Kat says. "Stella and I had a chat back when we first started planning this trip. The first thing she said was that she wanted you, Mara, to be on this trip with us even though she knew she wouldn't be joining us. The next thing she said was that we had to go to Bruges. Since we'd already suggested making it a day trip, it didn't take much convincing to add it as an end stop. She suggested a really cute B&B, and I have to tell you, it looks amazing."

"I can't wait for Bruges," Jo-Jo says. "It's been on my wish list for ages. Has anyone been?"

"Bruges? Stella specifically said that?" Lucy's voice sound a little harsh, almost even a little angry and Mara can't help but wonder why.

"She was very insistent on it, actually," Kat says with only a slight hesitation. "Is there a problem, Lucy?"

"What's the bed and breakfast called?" Lucy asks. There it is again, that anger.

"Lucy, is everything okay?" Mara keeps her voice low. "Is that... is that home?" She's never come right out and asked where Lucy is from, hoping that her friend will tell her along the way, when she's ready. She's not sure why keeping where she came from is such a big secret, but as Stella often reminded her, every woman has the right to keep her own secrets, and when and if Lucy is ready to tell hers, she will.

Lucy inhales sharply. "It is."

"What? Are you kidding me? Did Stella know?" Kat asks.

If Stella knew, she kept it a secret from Kat, that much is obvious.

"Oh, she knew." There's a hint of sadness in Lucy's voice, something deep, like a heartfelt sorrow she can't cover up. "She knew, and I think she planned all of this, to make sure...I know you have a lot of questions, Mara, and I know you want them answered, but..."

"That's a bit of an understatement," Mara says. She regrets the sarcasm added to her voice the second it comes out.

Lucy sighs. "The truth you're searching for isn't mine to tell. I wish I had a different answer for you, I do."

"Really?" Mara mutters. "Sure sounds like this is your story, Lucy. Why keep the fact Belgium is home to you a secret? I don't get it."

"Can someone explain what is going on?" Jo-Jo says the words everyone else is probably wondering.

Mara takes a long inhale and is about to answer when Alex returns.

Mara swallows her words, but not her frustration toward Lucy.

"All right, ladies. I've got your coffee. I'm placing it in the center of the table, with the cream and sugar containers beside it."

While they sip their coffees, Mara tells them about the letters, omitting most of what Lucy has told her about her own story, leaving that part to her - if she'll tell it.

The stunned silence justifies how Mara has been feeling since her video call with Lucy.

"I'm sorry to say this, but Mara, that sounds so crazy," Sandra says, clearing her throat.

"I know." It feels so good to have someone else say it.

"How are you doing with all this?" Kat asks. "I mean, losing your mom, then finding out about your father, and then coming on this trip - it's all a little much, right?"

Mara laughs. Not a good, funny, don't-you-know-it, laugh. More like an exhaustive, overwhelming, tell-me-about-it one instead.

"I can't wrap my head around it. I'm trying not to think about it, truth be told. I'm glad I'm here, that you all forced me to come. I want to just enjoy this trip, make the memories, think about how much Mom would have loved to be here...the other stuff, I don't even know how to feel about it." Her voice breaks a little. Thank goodness no one sees the tears that start to drip down her cheeks.

Jo-Jo squeezes her hand again, then pulls away. Moments later, she finds a tissue in her hand.

So, the tears were heard, even if not seen.

"What do you need from us?" Kat asks, always the practical one.

Mara smiles while she wipes the tears away. "I have no idea. Maybe help me celebrate Mom, I guess. The rest...I don't know what she expected to happen, to be honest. Did she think I would run into my father at a market?"

She looks toward Lucy, directing the question more to her than anyone else. She knows Lucy won't answer. She's been very vague about everything, only answering what was necessary and sharing the absolute minimum.

"Lucy, don't think we've forgotten about you. In all the years we've known each other, I don't think I ever knew you grew up in Belgium." Sandra says, her voice containing a little smile and many questions.

"That's a story for another time," Lucy says. "Ladies, I'm an old woman, and these old bones need to crawl into bed soon."

With that, they edge their way out from the table, let Alex guide them out of the dining area, and then make their way to the bathroom, where, surprisingly, there is hardly any chocolate on anyone's face or clothes.

"Well, that was fun. I'd do it again in a heartbeat. We should do something like that on our next trip." Lucy buttons up her coat and wraps a scarf around her neck. "You absolutely should do this for the store one night, Mara. Focus on a cookbook or a book with a chocolate theme...that would be fun, don't you think?"

"Now that we've done it, I agree. I still think doing it at Amy's diner would be fun, but as a book club idea, it would totally work. We have a local cookbook author who would be a great host." She's always trying to come up with fun events to do at the store and different book club ideas, and this would be perfect. The real issue would be making it dark enough.

"You might need to use blindfolds," Lucy says as if reading her thoughts.

Mara laughs. "And trust that people won't peek."

"Oh, I'd be peeking, but it would be so fun," Jo-Jo takes the lead and heads outside.

"Is everyone okay taking our time heading back, or would you prefer grabbing a taxi?" Kat directs the question more toward Lucy.

"It's a beautiful night, let's walk." Lucy says as she leads them along one of the canals. "Look at all the lights, it's like a fairytale, isn't it?"

Everyone is a little quiet as they make their way back to their hotel, taking in the sights, and stopping for picture-perfect photos.

It's not until they are in their room that Mara returns to the conversation about truths and who gets to tell them.

"Lucy, you said that the truth I'm looking for isn't yours to tell,"

"That's right." Lucy rummages around in her suitcase, not looking up.

"Then who's is it?"

Lucy slowly straightens and does a poor job of masking her surprise.

"Oh, sweetheart...that would rest with your mother."

Mara sighs. This is not the answer she's hoping for. "She's not exactly here, is she? Unless she told me in one of her letters? I'm trying to be patient and haven't asked too many questions, but I don't like being left in the dark, that's not fair," Mara says.

Lucy nods. "I hear you, I do." She inhales, her chest expanding with the action. "I think now is the time for another letter."

Mara doesn't say anything, not at first. The idea that her mother wrote her letters but Lucy gets to dole them out only at specific times, bothers her more than she wants to admit out loud.

Why wouldn't her mother trust her with the truth? Why parcel out the information in little sections? Her mother loved puzzles, but turning the truth into a puzzle, where she only gets one piece at a time, isn't right.

"No one holds ownership over the truth, Lucy. You said that once, do you remember?"

"I do," Lucy says. "I said that to your mother when we both thought you were downstairs, working. If we'd known you were home, the conversation wouldn't have come up, but as it was...you came in at the end of an argument over these very secrets your mother was keeping."

"Do you still believe it?"

"I do, honey. But I made promises that I can't break. If I'd known at the time the cost...I would never have agreed, I need you to believe that."

Without knowing the full truth, believing anything is hard.

Chapter Thirteen

Dear Mara-mine,

How frustrated are you with me?

Have you met Lucas yet?

There's something I need you to know about the man.

He's not a bad man. He's only a man who made a really bad mistake that I can never and will never forgive.

For years, I've wanted to blame him for what happened to me, to us, and for years, that's exactly what I did. I've blamed him for keeping your father from you. I've blamed him for being self-centered and self-focused for not caring about how his actions affect others.

I've blamed him for destroying the love I had for his son.

I swore I would never let the name of your father pass my lips, and I intend to keep it. I have no doubt you'll be angry with me about that, but darling...I've never been afraid of your anger.

Why won't I say his name? For the simple fact that he doesn't deserve it.

When he chose his parents over his unborn child, I saw a different side of him. A side I never expected to see.

He wasn't the man I thought he was, and I guess you could say that broke my heart.

Holding you in my arms repaired it. As soon as I saw you... nothing else mattered. I let go of the hatred and anger and realized we could live a life without them in it, and so that's what happened.

We lived our lives. You and me. Mother and daughter. We were all we ever needed, weren't we?

I did my best to make sure you never felt the loss of not having a father. You don't know what you're missing if you've never had it in the first place, right?

When you meet Lucas, I want you to remember something for me.

You can't miss what you never had.

Lucas made it very clear that you weren't important to him.

He was the one who told me to leave. He was the one who said I wasn't worthy of his son. He was the one who made your father choose between him and us.

There's a part of me that wants to tell you to be angry with him. But then that would mean accepting that the life we had was less than because he wasn't in it - and that's not true, is it?

He's not your grandfather, Mara. Don't let him tell you otherwise, either.

Don't let anyone tell you otherwise.

All the family we needed, we had. You. Me. Lucy and everyone else we surrounded ourselves with.

Don't let anyone convince you otherwise.

I love you.

Mom

Chapter Fourteen

Mara's running late, go figure.

After reading her mother's latest letter, she hardly slept a wink. While Lucy snored the night away, Mara tossed and turned. She kept thinking about what her mom had said - that you can't miss what you never had.

She's not sure if that's true. In fact, she knows it's not.

With these letters, Stella is playing dirty, even from the grave, and that's not fair.

She knows she keeps thinking that - that it's not fair - because it's the truth.

With everything inside her, she wishes Stella had the guts to tell her the truth before her death. She should have told her the truth a long time ago.

She feels betrayed by her mother, and that's not an emotion she's familiar with when it comes to Stella.

Frustrated. Angry. Resigned. Loved. Special. Treasured. Those she's familiar with.

Betrayal is a whole other level that Mara is struggling to grasp.

Lucy's downstairs enjoying her coffee and breakfast with the rest of the group, and even though Mara keeps getting messages to join them, she's in no hurry.

After the words she and Lucy had this morning, she's definitely not in a rush to see that woman.

She finishes packing up her toiletries from the bathroom when her phone rings and Nenita's cheerful face fills the screen as she accepts the video request.

"Hey, beautiful. I got your message and thought you needed a friend. How are you doing?"

Just hearing Nenita's voice is all Mara needs to feel some semblance of calmness. She lets out a sigh, pushing away all the frustration and resentment building around her heart.

"What time is it for you?" Mara tries to count backward, with them being eight hours ahead. "You're normally in bed by now, aren't you?"

"That's Chris. Ten o'clock, and it's lights out for him. He's been like this our whole life. Me…I'm normally up until past twelve reading, so it being eleven at night is nothing. You should know me better than that … this is now officially 'me' time."

Nenita is right. Mara can't count how many of their text conversations happened between ten and midnight.

"I wish you were here," Mara says. "One day, maybe we can go on a trip together." She knows the chance of that is slim, but she says it nonetheless.

"For that to happen, my dear husband will need to be six feet in the dirt," Nenita confirms, "and as much as he drives me bananas some days, I'm not ready for that."

"Yeah, I get that. Maybe a day trip then, for now?" She suggests. Day trips with Nenita are always fun, even if it's just on a dollar-store spree in the city for holiday decorations or a run to Ikea for furniture. "Sorry for the ranting message I left you last night, I just needed to get it out before Lucy was out of the shower. Otherwise, she would have gotten the brunt of my feelings, and that wouldn't be fair to her."

"But it's fair to me?" Nenita asks.

Mara winces.

"Kidding, seriously," Nenita says. "You know I'm always here, no judgments from me. Vent as much as you need. I kind of like being your safe place."

Mara smiled at the phrasing, recognizing it from something she'd said in her voicemail.

"To recap that message you left, your mother dropped another truth bomb about a man named Lucas. A man who, according to your mother is not your father, instead, he's your grandfather, except your mom doesn't want you calling him that, much less thinking of him like that."

"That about sums it up."

"And Lucy's mute on any explanations?"

"Yep."

Nenita sighs. "That woman can be frustrating on the best of days. And you're headed to her hometown in a few days, something Stella set up with Kat?"

Mara nods, then runs her hand through her hair, feeling vexed.

"I barely slept a wink last night; all I could think about was all this. My father. Mom's secrets. Whatever secrets Lucy seems to be hiding…it's all too much, Nenita. I almost wish I hadn't come; you know? And I know there are more letters, but I'm thinking maybe I don't want them. Is that wrong?" Her voice hitches at the question as she realizes how honest she's being right now.

No more huge revealings. No more games. That would be so nice.

"You know," Nenita says, her voice hinting at something Mara knows she's not going to like. "It's really not right for Stella to manipulate you like that, especially now."

Manipulate. Mara didn't like that word, especially regarding her mother. "Mom wasn't manipulating me," she says, defending a dead woman who can't speak up for herself. "She was just… reminding me, I guess."

"She was telling you how to feel, darling. Your mother was amazing, but she was no saint. She's had complete control over your past until now. Are you going to let her continue to have that tight hold?"

Mara opens her mouth to argue, then closes it. She's struggling with how to feel toward Stella right now. Of course, she's angry and upset, frustrated, and if Stella were here, and if she were able to process her actions, Mara would be very plain with her words.

But she's not. And the truth is, Mara hasn't been able to explore all her emotions for the past few years, mainly because it wouldn't be fair to her mother.

The dementia wasn't her fault. The need for care wasn't her fault either. Losing her memories, forgetting her own daughter...none of that blame can be laid at Stella's feet, so Mara did the only thing she could do. She held everything in until she's an outsider when it comes to experiencing her own emotions.

Even now. Even with these letters and Lucy's secrets and the constant grief that is always right there...there's a distance between how she should be feeling and how she actually feels. Like a wide gulf extending between the two, Mara is stuck in the middle of the water with no paddle.

"What's this trip about? Beyond the Christmas markets and all the amazing chocolate you're bringing home for me to taste?" Nenita asks with a smile in her voice.

It doesn't take long for Mara to respond. "It's about finding out the truth." The words pop out of her mouth without thought.

"Exactly. So do that. Use what Stella tells you in her letters, and then determine the path you want to take. Not the one anyone else suggests, the one you want to take."

"And what if I don't know the direction to go?"

"Listen to your gut, honey."

"I'm trying, but Lucy—"

"Lucy has her own agenda, as much as I hate to say it. It sounds like she knows more than she's willing to tell you."

Bingo. Nenita hits it on the head. "She says she can't."

Nenita shakes her head. "You're giving her the easy way out. It sounds more like she's decided not to. Lucy is a grown woman with a mind of her own, and for the little I know of her, she's not one to let others tell her what to do or even what to say."

"That's true."

"I know." There's a hint of smugness in Nenita's voice.

"I feel so...stressed? Overwhelmed? Anxious? Does that even make sense?"

"Of course it does. You're playing tag while blinded, love. That's not enjoyable in the least. Besides, you haven't truly given ownership to your own feelings for a while now, and don't bother telling me I'm wrong."

Everything Nenita is saying is true. "So what do I do? How do I deal with all this? I mean...I don't want this trip ruined because of my insecurities or fears, you know?"

"Try to enjoy the moments, Mara. That's all you can do. Take each one as it comes; don't look at the looming future of uncertainty, exist in the now." Nenita's words hit home in a very real way. "Enjoy all that Christmas spirit around you, especially the chocolate," she continues. "Walk those cobbled streets without twisting an ankle and fill your phone storage with all the photos you'll show me when you return. You don't have to let this trip be ruined because of the secrets."

Secrets. There's that word again, and it rips her right out of the mood she is starting to feel.

"It's kind of hard knowing there's a grandfather out there who wanted nothing to do with me."

"Bah humbug. Put him out of your head. What's the chance you'll run into him, anyway? Why give him a room in your heart and mind when he doesn't deserve it? Put him out of your mind if you can."

"That's easier said than done, Nenita, and you know it." Mara rubs her forehead.

"It would bug the heck out of me, too, but try not to let it."

"I'll try." Mara's not sure how well that will work, but who knows, it might. Or not.

"Listen, there's something I want to say to you, something that's bothering me. It's that part where Stella says your father didn't choose you." Nenita pauses, looking off to the side. "Mara, every child, every person, deserves to be chosen, and even though you didn't know the man, I'm sure that hurt to read."

Hurt is an understatement, even though Mara tries her best not to let that invade her thoughts or heart.

Nothing in her life has changed since reading that letter. She still doesn't know her father and still has no concept of what it would be like to have him in her life, so there's nothing for that info to affect. Right?

Except it does.

"Mom said you can't miss what you never had. Do you think that's true?"

Nenita shrugs. "That's kind of hard to grasp, don't you think? You don't know you're missing something until it's pointed out to you, but once you feel that void, does it ever disappear?

Exactly.

She never thought about why her father wasn't in her life. In fact, she never thought about not having a father. There just wasn't one. It was simple, straightforward, and all she ever needed to know as a child. But now, knowing he didn't want her, that he didn't choose her or them...it stings on so many levels, more than Mara is even aware of. She's not sure how to feel or react or...

No. That's a lie. She feels hurt. She feels sad. And there's a tiny part of her that feels unwanted.

That's a gut-kick in itself.

She's never felt that way before. Her mother worked hard to ensure she always knew she was loved and wanted. Now, to find out that someone who should have wanted her the most, other than Stella, didn't...she can't even wrap her head around how to process that.

A text message from Lucy pops up on Mara's display. "Lucy says if we don't hurry, we'll miss the train. Guess that's my cue... thanks Nenita, for listening and always being there."

"Always. We're family, hun, don't you ever forget that. Chat soon...I want to hear all about Brussels and Bruges. Chris and I were looking at photos online today, and wow, it's like a fairytale town. Make sure you visit the Grand Place, or whatever it's called, at night. The buildings light up to music; from what we saw online, it's magical."

"I think I'm more excited about Bruges, to be honest. It's a town with over fifty chocolate shops." On the way back to the hotel, Kat told them about the chocolate walk she has planned.

"Then I expect at least one side of your carry-on luggage to be full of chocolate for us to enjoy."

One side? Does Nenita honestly think that's all she'd buy?

Mara brought a compact bag that she plans on filling with the treats. Nothing tastes better than chocolate made in Europe.

Chapter Fifteen

The train ride from Amsterdam to Brussels is quiet, with everyone lost in their own thoughts or enjoying a quick nap.

While the scenery passes, Mara keeps rereading those words in her mother's letter over and over...she knows she should focus on something else, anything else, so she can enjoy the views of the small towns they pass and the quaint houses dotting the landscape, but they pass by in a whirlwind.

Lucy seems to be lost in her own thoughts as well. Anytime Mara thinks to start up a conversation between them, one glance at Lucy, with how she sits in her seat, eyes closed, hands held tight together in her lap, and she changes her mind.

Lucy seems to be battling her own demons, and as much as she should reach out to make sure her friend is okay, she doesn't.

Lucy's the type that if she wants to share something, she will. Otherwise, good luck getting anything out of her.

Arriving in Brussels feels like a gong show with the swirl of crowds around them. With their luggage trailing behind them on the narrow, cobbled streets, it seems like almost everyone is in a sour mood, especially Kat.

"Sorry guys," she says as they walk through the doors of their hotel. "I honestly thought it was closer."

"As long as the wheels don't break," Sandra says as she stares at her suitcase, "it's all fine. Besides, it wasn't that far of a walk, there's just way too many people on the sidewalks."

"I told Stephanie it didn't matter, but," her lips thin as her chest heaves. "I just need coffee or wine, and something to eat." Kat leads them all to the front desk so they can check into their rooms.

"Belgium is small enough that we could just do day trips," Lucy says. "Why don't we see if we can extend our stay here?"

Kat shakes her head. "The B&B in Bruges is prepaid, and we're past the cancellation date. I can look about getting a private transfer, though, if you'd like?"

Lucy waves the suggestion away. "It's cheaper and makes more sense to take the train. It's fine." She may say it's fine, but Mara can tell it's not. Something inside Lucy has closed off. She's pushing everyone away, little by little, and she probably doesn't even realize it.

Sensing her friend needs some space, Mara fixes a smile on her face, but keeps all thoughts and comments to herself as they head to their room. They've all agreed to meet in the cafe across from the hotel for a glass of wine, so Mara drops her bags off and heads there early, telling Lucy to come when she's ready.

She's the first one and grabs two tables outside beneath heaters. A street artist plays a guitar off to the side and gives her a smile as he catches her watching him. She notices a couple from a few tables over being served mounded cups of what looks like hot cocoa with whipped cream.

She decides to order something similar, which turns out to be a Baileys Hot Cocoa, and when it arrives, the first thing Mara does is wrap her hands around the mug. There's nothing better than the warmth coming from the cup, especially on a cool winter day.

"Oh, this is cozy." Sandra is the first to join her. "And that looks delicious. Here, let me take a photo and see if we should just order one for everyone." She takes a few snaps and sends it off. By the time the server returns, they order one for everyone except for Lucy, who says she's going to take a nap and will meet up with everyone later.

Mara sends her a private reply, checking in and making sure she's okay. Maybe she shouldn't have left so quick, maybe she should have stuck around in the room and invaded Lucy's space.

"I'm worried about Lucy, she's right in the thick of things. This trip, she seems off, which I guess is understandable, considering everything." Sandra leans back in her chair and rummages through her purse. "I saw something the other day and grabbed it for you," she says, biting her lip as she pulls out one item after the other.

Intrigued, Mara watches as her friend finally pulls out a magnet in the shape of a chocolate bar.

"Here it is. It's kitschy, but..." she shrugs as she hands it over.

I can face all things as long as there's chocolate, is written on what looks like a chocolate bar wrapper.

"This is cute," Mara says, giving her friend a side hug. It'll look perfect beside the other similar chocolate magnets covering her fridge door. Collecting magnets was Stella's thing, but the fact Sandra thought of her means the world.

"I hate being the one to ask because I know everyone probably asks the same thing, but are you okay? Honestly?" Sandra asks.

Holding the cup with one hand and playing with the whipped cream with her spoon, Mara thinks about how to answer.

"Am I okay? I guess that depends on the day or maybe even the moment. I mean...I'm doing, if that means anything." She won't look at Sandra even though she knows she should. Being vulnerable is hard. For the past few years, her focus has been on Stella and making sure she was okay. All her energy, her emotional stability, her...everything...was centered around her mother's illness. Now that that's gone...

"My whole world is gone, you know? I lived for Mom. I had no other choice." There, the words are out. Will that be enough?

"That hasn't changed, has it?"

Mara looks at her friend then. "What do you mean?" Of course, it's changed. Stella is gone.

"Although, I'm sure you still need time," Sandra continues as if she didn't hear Mara's question. "It takes time to adjust, to rediscover who you are, remembering who you were before Stella's need for your help became all-consuming." The head tilt from Sandra as if she's getting a glance inside Mara's soul and wants to see deeper, is unsettling.

Sandra used to be a social worker, so it's no surprise. She's also lost her spouse, so if anyone in the group understands what it means to find life and oneself after a close death, it would be her.

"How long did it take for you?" Mara asks.

Sandra's smile is swallowed by sadness. "If it weren't for you girls and my church, I'm sure I'd still be struggling to answer that. You might feel alone, but you're not."

The server arrives with the other four drinks just as the girls all arrive.

"I hope that tastes just as good as it looks," Kat says, taking a seat.

"Can I get you ladies anything else?" the server asks.

"Should we get some of those famous Belgian fries?" Kat asks the group. Without waiting for a reply, she shines a smile upward. "Will one order be enough?"

Their server nods. "I'll grab you a large with some extra dip."

"So what did we miss?" Jo-Jo asks as she sets her purse on the table. "I really should have brought one of those hooks where you hang your bag, you know? It's not safe to hang our purses on the back of chairs, and I'm certainly not placing my bag on the dirty ground."

"I was just checking in on our girl." Sandra gives Mara a quick glance. "You're all interrupting our little heart-to-heart." She winks as she lifts up her mug and sips, getting a dab of whipped cream on her nose.

"So, what's the verdict?" Donna moves her seat so she's not facing outward and away from the others. "I'm all for people watching, but I like to see your faces too," she says when she notices everyone giving her a raised brow.

"The verdict," Mara says, "is that I haven't had time to think about it, you know? It's only been a few weeks since the funeral. Between this trip and then Mom's bombshell..." she shakes her head. "I don't know how I am or how I feel, and you know me... having to share that isn't really one of my strongest suits." One side of her lip turns upward as she shrugs.

"I was telling Mara that you girls were my saving grace after Jeff passed away." Sandra leans to the side and places her head on Kat's shoulder. "Whenever I thought I'd lose myself in my grief, one of you was always there. You didn't try to fix me or give me pathetic platitudes, you were just there. Knowing I wasn't alone, that's what helped. Having your love and support, you guys have no idea what that meant for me. I want her to know we've got her back."

Mara blinks hard to fight the tears that swell. "Come on guys," she says, picking up a napkin and dabbing at her eyes. "My mascara is fresh, and I'm not exploring Brussels with black runs down my face."

"Talking about Christmas Markets, I did a little online search, do you know that even people who live in Belgium love to come to the markets here? I even found a map that will hit all the major ones if we follow it in a circular pattern." Kat says. "We'll start at the Grand-Place and then end there. The sound and lights display is going to be spectacular. They apparently change it up every year and use different music. Jo-Jo," Kat glances over at the woman taking a photo of her drink, "that would be a great one to video and post."

"Consider it done. As of now, I'm the official photographer of our trip, okay?" She turns her phone around and shows off the picture she took.

"I wish Lucy were joining us." Mara checks her phone to see if Lucy has responded to any of her texts, making sure she's doing okay, but so far, there's nothing. Maybe she did lie down for a nap.

"I feel kind of bad," Kat admits. "When Stella asked me to make some changes to our itinerary, I had no idea the personal connection for Lucy."

"Yeah, but you also didn't expect Lucy to come. She was supposed to stay behind with Stella, so you can't take the blame for that." Donna says.

"True. But still...I wish Stella had been more honest with me about things. She was insistent that we go to Bruges. I mean, like crazy insistent. She wouldn't let up until I promised her. I figured it was part of her dementia, but..." her voice trails off as she glances toward Mara with a question.

"I have no idea, guys. Mom was...well, you all know. Most of the time, she lived in a past I wasn't familiar with. I wasn't even her daughter, just some roommate to help with the bills..." she shrugs her shoulder. "I never knew if what she remembered was her actual past or one she created for herself. She never mentioned my father, though, which, if she were living in her past, you think she would have, right?"

Round and round, Mara's thoughts journey, in no pattern, and with no answers. All there are are questions, questions that no one has answers to. It's frustrating.

"Can I ask a favor?" Mara sits up straight and pushes her empty cup forward on the table. "No more talk of what I'm going through, of my mom's crazy letters or whatever she had planned, okay? Let's enjoy Brussels and do some Christmas shopping. I, for one, want to see what type of glasses they're using for their gluwein, and Kat, didn't you mention you had a list of chocolate shops we have to visit?"

By the time they leave the cafe, Mara is in a better mood. She sends Lucy a quick message, letting her know they started walking, and even snaps a photo of Kat's map she made in case Lucy wants to find them later.

Chapter Sixteen

From the wooden chalet stands to the warm apple cider in their boot-shaped market mug found by the ice skating rink in De Brockere, the Brussels Christmas Market lived up to its hype. Every woman in the group had items in their shopping bags, but Mara found the best item of all.

While Jo-Jo buys candy from a vendor, Mara notices a chalet with a Canadian flag. She heads on over and notices the samples of both authentic Canadian maple sugar candy and whiskey. Glancing around to see if anyone notices where she went, she waves for Sandra to join her.

"Of course, the Canadian would find a Canadian whiskey in Belgium," Sandra teases.

"Have you ever tried it?" Mara asks, picking up a sample cup. There are two types to choose from, one being a cream version. "You know I love maple syrup, but I've never tried a maple whiskey."

She samples the cream whiskey first and is amazed at how smooth it goes down.

"Oh girl..." Sandra says after she finishes her sample. "I used to think Vermont had the best maple syrup, but this...this is a whole new level."

"What are we enjoying?" Jo-Jo shows up and takes an offered sample without hesitation. "Who would pass up free whiskey, right?"

One by one, everyone is there, circled around the samples. Mara picks up a brochure, making a mental note to see where she can buy this at home. She grabs two sample bottles, an original and a cream. There's no way these bottles are making it home, but after talking to the vendor, she knows that's not an issue. Sure enough, a local liquor store back at home sells this brand.

"Now that I'm feeling all warm and cozy inside, I overheard someone mention a Bailey's stand around the corner and I know how much both you and Stella loved your Bailey's. Especially that chocolate one you can only buy in Europe." Kat wiggles her brows as she tugs on Mara's arm.

"Mom loved her Baileys," Mara says with a smile. Stella loved to add a splash or dash of Bailey's into most things - like cakes, cake frosting, brownies, mousse, hot chocolate, or even sip it on its own. There was always an opened bottle in the fridge and one on reserve in the cupboard.

Sure enough, they find the Chocolate Lux flavor Mara loves. She wishes she could get it back home, but so far, the only place they've ever found it was in Germany or at the duty-free shops in the European airports. One sip of the velvety goodness, and you're transported to chocolate heaven as the silk dream sits on your tongue and wraps you in its warm, welcoming hug.

Everyone buys a small bottle. Mara grabs an extra one for Lucy, knowing the woman would love the drink. Jo-Jo, of course, orders a box and pays for it to be shipped back home.

"It's times like this I wish I'd brought a larger suitcase," Mara mutters. There's no way she could bring a bottle back in her carry-on.

A Belgium Chocolate Christmas

"Are you from America? They're now available in stores there," says the woman in the booth as she leans forward.

"What?" This is news to Mara. "They are, but I'm from Canada."

The woman frowns. "Oh, that's too bad. Hopefully, soon, you'll get it there. I haven't heard of a release day yet, though. But, you should try the airports here before you head home, you'll for sure be able to find them there."

As they walk away, Kat looks at her map. "Okay, ladies. It's close to dinner time, so I think now is the perfect time to start our chocolate walk. I've been in touch with Lucy, and she's going to join us along the way."

She leads the way back to the Grand-Place and stops in front of a chocolate shop with a cute display in its front window. There's a small Christmas tree decorated with hanging chocolate balls, and the base is full of different boxed chocolates, including an advent calendar.

"Neuhaus is the oldest chocolate shop in Brussels, so of course, we have to start here," Kat says. "It used to be a pharmacy back in the eighteen hundreds. The owner wanted an inventive way for his clients to take their medicines, so he covered them with chocolate. They also created the praline, which I think is Mara's favorite chocolate, correct me if I'm wrong?"

Mara smiles. "You're not wrong. I fully intend to find some hazelnut paste and bring it home with me. Eating that stuff by the spoonful is better than sex itself." She gives Kat a wink, and while her tone might be jovial, she's one hundred percent serious. Every other year, when they come on their market tours, she makes a point to find and buy all the hazelnut paste she can find from chocolate shops. It's like eating a Ferrero Roche but better.

"Then you'll want to try one of their Cornet Dores. It's one of their specialties and resembles a small ice cream cone," Kat instructs.

Their next stop is a few doors down, called Mary Chocolatier.

"Oh, we've been in one of these before. Wasn't it in Paris, maybe?" Jo-Jo says.

Kat nods. "I bought some of their baking cocoa and need more. Did you know she was Brussels' first female chocolatier?"

Mara makes a point to buy a few extra pieces while inside the shop. She loves the feminine vibe with its pastel colors. She grabs a few truffles in honor of her mom and then a few extra praline chocolates for herself.

Lucy joins them while they're still inside. "Oh, I love Mary's," she says.

"Did you have a nice nap?" Mara asks her after placing her purchases in her bag.

"The quiet time was nice and what I needed," Lucy says as she peers into Mara's bag. "Looks like you found some treats."

"I did and even picked up something for you." She hands her the Bailey's, and as Lucy's smile grows along her face, she knows she made the right choice. "It's also an apology gift. You seemed a little unsettled with me."

The shock of surprise on Lucy's face is comforting. "You? Goodness, no. I warned you I'd have moments, and honestly, finding out we're headed to my hometown was just a little much for me. I haven't been back in a…long time." She glances away, and Mara watches as sadness combined with resolve marches across the woman's face. "Anyhoo, I don't want to talk about that right now, okay? I'd much rather buy some of those champagne truffles I see in the display."

They walk while enjoying their chocolates, stopping at a cookie shop before making their way down Rue de l'Etuve when they see a crowd up ahead.

"I bet that's where the statue of Manneken-Pis is," Kat says.

"Is he the little pissing boy?" Jo-Jo asks. "Didn't he put out a fire while peeing on it, saving a castle or something?"

"I think that's one of the legends. He has a sister somewhere, too."

They pause for photos before continuing on until Kat stops them at a two-story shop for Pierre Marcolini.

"I love playing tour guide," Kat says as she pulls out her phone. "This guy started as a pastry chef before he became a chocolatier. Apparently, this is the place for luxurious chocolate. The first level is where we buy the chocolates, but ladies, we're heading upstairs for a chocolate tasting first."

After a solid thirty minutes in that store, they continue their walk until they come to a shopping area called Les Galeries Royales Saint-Hubert. After a little bit of window shopping, they leave and continue their walk.

Dazzling Christmas lights are strung all around the shops, and light posts, and they shine brighter as the sun sets. Up ahead, a street artist plays a lovely Christmas song on her violin, and Mara watches as couples walk along the streets, hand in hand.

She's never been one to miss not being in a relationship. She's had a few, one that held potential, but she always felt like there was something more, something she was missing, and if she settled, she'd be closing the door to something even better. But seeing these couples, she wonders if maybe she truly is missing out on something. Now that she's alone, who else can she share her wanderlust spirit with? Sure, she has the ladies, but they all have their own families to focus on. And yes, she has Lucy, but Lucy has her own life, too.

What is it going to be like going back home to an empty apartment?

She'll throw herself into the holiday season at the store and work all the hours she can, but what about after Christmas? When the crazy season is behind her, and she won't need to work those extra hours?

Will the quietness in her place become too much?

"You're awfully quiet all of a sudden," Lucy says as she winds her arm through Mara's. "What's going on in that head of yours?"

Mara sighs as she pulls her gaze away from the couple up

ahead. "Thinking too much about the future and letting fear and worry sink in, that's all."

Lucy pulls her in tighter. "I promised I'd remind you to focus on the now and not the when, so here's me, saying, smarten up." The smile in her voice softens her words. "I think you need another piece of chocolate," she says.

"Kat, are we stopping anywhere else before dinner?" Lucy calls out.

Kat turns around and nods. "We have one more chocolate shop that I thought might be interesting to visit, then we're headed to an Italian place where they make their noodles fresh every day, according to the reviews."

"There we go," Lucy says to Mara. "Chocolate, pasta, and wine. Doesn't that sound perfect? Maybe a little out of order, but," she shrugs as if saying who cares?

Mara agrees. The forced smile she pastes on her face becomes natural as they continue their walk, with Lucy humming carols under her breath.

Be in the now and not the when. Mara likes that.

Along Rue au Beurre is a rustic and unassuming chocolate shop called Le Comptoir de Mathilde. It's full of chocolate souvenirs, including hot cocoa spoons, magnets, and even pots of salted caramel. Mara finds a bin full of slabs of chocolate with Rice Krispie kernels. She picks out a pre-packaged bag that comes with a little mallet to smash the slabs into smaller pieces and then grabs a magnet in honor of her mother.

Mara glances around the shop at her girlfriends and realizes it's not hard to be in the now with them.

Remembering Stella, enjoying the things she knows her mother would have loved, making memories that she hopefully won't one day forget, that's what being in the now means.

Chapter Seventeen

From the moment she woke up, she knew today was not going to be a good day.

First, there's the headache, thanks to the copious wine and spirits they drank as a group last night.

The fact her roommate woke up on the wrong side of the bed doesn't help either.

Mara escaped their room to head to breakfast and met with others suffering the same hangover.

Note to self: don't drink like that again. She's too old for that nonsense. And if she's too old, the others are absolutely way over that limit, too, although she'd never say that to their faces.

By the time they depart their hotel and make it to the Midi station, it seems like everyone in the group feels the same overwhelming stress that hits Mara like a bag full of marbles.

As they navigate the floor to find the correct platform for Bruges, she's surprised by the chaos within the station. "Is it always like this?" She directs the question to Lucy, which is a mistake.

"How would I know? Do you know how long it's been since I've been back?" Lucy's tone bites, and while Mara wants to snap back, she doesn't, mainly because she hears something in Lucy's voice that stops her.

"I'm sorry, that was uncalled for," Lucy apologizes.

She needs to be gentler with the woman. No doubt she's a ball of nerves going back home.

Lucy rubs the back of her neck, then forces something that doesn't look anything like a true smile on her face. "It's the holiday season, a weekend, and everyone is coming to enjoy the markets. No wonder it is so crazy," Lucy mutters as they watch a group of police walk by, hands on the guns slung over their shoulders.

"I'm sorry this is so hard on you." Mara reaches out and lightly touches Lucy's hand. "You don't have to come. You could go to Paris or London or..." she repeats something she brought up this morning.

Lucy purses her lips together and shakes her head. "Enough with that talk. Whatever happens will happen," she says. "Now, let's figure out our platform, shall we?"

Kat stands in front of the large schedule display. "Um, Lucy, I'm not seeing a train for Bruges. Was it canceled?"

Lucy shakes her head. "I doubt it. They have trains departing every hour or so. It's right there - platform nine to Oostende. It'll stop in Bruges, don't worry."

Mara checks her watch. They have at least a forty-five-minute wait. Standing in the middle of the room with swelling crowds bumping into her is not ideal, even with a firm grip on her luggage and purse, so she navigates her way to a bench and looks around.

There are quite a few stores here, from chocolate shops to pharmacies, cafes, and places to grab a coffee and sandwich to go.

Mara keeps an eye on the scheduler and notices their train information disappears.

"Um, Lucy," she points. "What happened to our train?"

Lucy gets up and walks closer, leaving her luggage with Mara. She stands there for a few minutes, then steps back. "It's all good, nothing major to worry about. We'll grab a different train, which should be arriving soon. Come on, we need to head to platform twelve."

They all make their way to the escalator and join a crowded platform with others to wait.

"What about our tickets, though?" Jo-Jo asks, her voice showcasing the misgivings she's feeling. "Will we be forced to pay a hefty fine once someone checks our tickets after we're already on the train?" She looks from Kat to Lucy as she worries her lip.

The frustration on Lucy's face disappears. "We're fine, Jo-Jo. I promise. Our ticket is good for the day on any train in Belgium. Some will take longer than others, with more stops along the way, but generally, they're all about the same. This one heads to Ghent, with a stop in Bruges."

A few of the girls go to sit on a bench while Mara and Lucy stand off to the side. Lucy's focused on her phone, and Mara stares at the notice board, waiting to see how long till their train arrives, when a family with a plethora of luggage brushes past and plops their stuff down.

"I hope we're on the right train," the woman says. She directs her husband and two older children to place their extensive luggage off the side.

"Where are you heading to?" Lucy looks up from her phone and over at the woman.

"Bruges."

"So are we," Mara says, a smile alighting on her face.

"Oh, good. I was so worried, and the stations aren't clearly marked."

"We should have done a private transfer," one of the boys spoke up.

"At those prices? I think not." The man Mara assumes is the husband/father mutters as he sits down on an empty bench beside their luggage and pulls out his own phone.

"I'm Lucy, and this is Mara." Lucy introduces them. "Are you…Canadian or American, by chance?" The extrovert in action,

Lucy places her phone in her purse and glances at all the luggage. "On a ski trip, I'm assuming?" For the four of them, there are at least ten pieces of luggage, ranging from carry-ons to large suitcases, hard shell cases for what has to be skis and poles, along with obvious helmet shells.

"American, west coast. We're headed to Switzerland in a few days to join the rest of our family. My husband had business in Brussels first, so we came a little early. I've always wanted to see the Bruges market, I hear it's one not to miss…but when I was booking all the tickets, I didn't think about all the extra luggage we'd be bringing with us." She quirks her lips before giving a slight eye roll. "And yes," she looks toward one son, "Eric is right. We should have paid for a private transfer. We will on the return trip, that's for sure."

"Oh, so are we, going to the market, I mean," Mara speaks up and points to the group sitting on the bench next to them. "We do this every couple of years, the markets in Europe," she continues, knowing she's speaking too much and saying nothing necessary. She glances at Lucy, who's giving her a strange look.

"There's what, six of you? And you do this all the time? That would be fun." The woman says.

"Despite the luggage issue, you are going to love Bruges," Lucy offers.

"Hey, hun, I just got a WhatsApp message from the hotel. Asking if we'd like a transfer from the station?"

The woman glances over at Lucy. "Have you been to Bruges before? We're staying at The Pand Hotel."

Lucy's eyes light up. "I grew up in Bruges. If The Pand Hotel is offering you a transfer," she glances over at their luggage, "I'd take them up on it. You can grab a taxi from the station, but they'll charge extra for the luggage."

"Thank you. I'm Robin, by the way, I don't think I introduced myself or my crew. That's my husband Ken and two of our boys,

Eric and Jordan. My two daughters and their husbands are meeting us in Switzerland."

"Four children, you are an amazing woman," Lucy says.

"More like tired, still, even though Jordan is the only one left at home now. I don't think our bodies ever acclimate to motherhood. My doctor once said my body will forever be in a perpetual state of exhaustion, that there's no making up for the lack of sleep, constant stress..." she stops and chuckles. "I can see from the smile on your face, you understand what I'm saying."

Lucy laughs. "Well, I don't have children, but I am dealing with age, so I understand the exhaustion you feel. My advice? Enjoy all the coffee and chocolate you want if that helps put a pep in your step. We don't have time for regrets, not anymore."

Robin nods. "I hear you on that."

"Hey, Mom, is that our train?" One of Robin's boys pokes his head up from the phone he's been engrossed in and points down the line.

Robin glances toward Lucy, who nods. "Looks like it," she says. She nudges her husband with her foot. "This will take us right to Bruges, so we're almost done with the luggage fiasco."

As the train pulls up, Robin and her family struggle to get all their luggage together, slinging things over their shoulders, and stacking them on top of other luggage.

"Oh dear," Robin mumbles as the train stops, and she realizes it has split-level seating.

"You go ahead of us," Ken says, standing out of the way. "They won't leave us behind, right? Not if they see us trying to get our stuff on board?"

"They shouldn't," Lucy says in a hopeful voice.

"Where's the luggage section?" The desperation in Robin's voice ups a notch.

"This is a commuter train, so there won't be," Lucy says. "Here, let us help. Mara...can you go in and see if one section would be better over the other?"

Mara waits until the crowds ahead of her enter the train. First, she heads upstairs but sees right away, there is no seating. She hurries down to the lower compartment, giving Lucy a thumbs up out of a window. If everyone hurries, there's more than enough room down here.

It takes time, but they're able to stick things in the overhead racks or on empty seats around them.

"Finally. This is a little ridiculous if I'm being honest." Robin says as she sits beside her husband.

Mara and her group all sit on the opposite side of the train. "Think we should have a nap before we head out this afternoon?" She suggests to Kat.

"A nap and coffee is a definite plan. Good thinking."

Lucy glances over toward the family. "You must be excited about your ski trip," directing her comment to Robin.

"I'll be excited once we're actually there," Ken mutters before he turns around and talks with their sons.

"The boys had a late night," Robin says. "Ken and Eric work for the same company, and they didn't get back to the hotel last night until quite late. I think Eric has a bit of food poisoning from the business dinner last night, too. The boys want to get to the hotel and take a nap, while Jordan and I head to the markets." She pulls out a Rick Steve's travel guide. "We're only here for a few days, and there's so much I want to see and do, and there's no way I'm spending time in the hotel room, waiting for them to have their nap," she says.

Halfway to their destination, an announcement over the speakers has everyone in a panic.

"What's going on?" Mara asks Lucy.

Lucy listens for a little bit with a frown on her face.

"We have to get off the train at the next station and take another. Apparently, there's a tree on the tracks up ahead."

"A tree?"

Lucy shrugs. "Something about a storm last night, and the tree fell about an hour ago." She heaves a sigh. "As if this day couldn't get any better."

"At least we're not in a rush, right?" Sandra covers her mouth with a yawn. "I hope that B&B has comfy beds. It felt like I slept on rocks all night."

"Lucy, we have to get off?" Robin leans across the chairs. "Is everything okay?"

"We need to transfer to a different train and do a little backtracking, nothing to worry about."

"How long is the delay?"

The voice overhead comes on again, and everyone pauses to listen.

"Probably an hour in total," Lucy says.

As they pull into the station, Robin and Ken start to gather their stuff and make their way toward the doors.

"We should help them," Mara says quietly.

Lucy nods.

Together, the six of them help carry the helmets, balancing the cases on their own luggage while they carefully maneuver from one train to the other. Thankfully, they were right across the tracks, so it was an easy transfer.

Unfortunately, the train they board is packed, with no room to sit. The Batterson family pushes their way through the crowds, trying to find room, while Mara and her group all squeeze into the alcove by the doors. They stand shoulder to shoulder, with Mara's leg tight up against a bicycle.

The train reminds her of a time when she was visiting New York City during rush hour. There'd been barely any standing room in the subway car, and at that time, Mara had been pushed tight against the doors.

Lucy starts speaking to someone beside her, then turns to Mara with a sigh. "So, this train stops at the next station, which means we need to transfer again."

"Oh no. And Robin and her family aren't anywhere close for

us to tell them." Mara tries to look down the cart but can't see them anywhere.

"They'll figure it out. Bet you are happy we only brought carry-ons, aren't you?" Lucy asks.

Donna and Jo-Jo both groan. "Stop rubbing it in our faces, okay?"

Mara gives her friend a smile before turning to Lucy with a bit of a saucy grin. "Can you imagine? Lugging a heavy suitcase on and off the trains, carrying them up the stairs to the platforms...no thank you."

They manage to navigate their way off the train at the next station, climb down stairs, rush across the station, then back up another set of stairs to the platform where their train waits. Mara tries to keep an eye out for the other family and finally sees them down the platform. She lifts her hand in greeting even though they aren't paying her any attention.

They find seating on an upper floor and sink down in their chairs. No one says much as the train leaves the station.

Mara glances over at Kat and notices a frown on the woman's face as she reads something on her phone.

"Everything okay?"

Kat looks up. "It's fine. I had arranged a ride from the station, but because our schedule changed, we'll need to take a taxi."

"That's not an issue, right?" Mara asks.

"No. I need to make sure we'll get a refund, that's all."

"Kat," Lucy says, leaning forward. "I really need to know the name of the B&B we're going to."

"Oh, I thought I already told you. Sorry, Lucy, it must have slipped my mind. We're going to the Barabas Bed and Breakfast."

Lucy sits back in her seat with a thud. "You've got to be kidding me."

"Do you know it?" The hesitation in Kat's voice is real and full of misgiving.

Something inside Mara's stomach twists.
"Know it? That's my family home."

Chapter Eighteen

"I'm sorry, what?" Mara asks, praying to God she didn't hear Lucy right.

"I had no idea, Lucy, honestly. Stella was—"

"I know."

"If I'd—"

"It's okay, Kat. You didn't know. This is all on Stella." Lucy's tone makes it very clear just how unhappy she is with the news. "That woman..." her voice trails off as she pulls out her phone.

"Guess I should let them know I'm coming home," she says with a sigh. She glances at Mara but the look in her gaze is shuttered.

She has so many questions, so many things she wants to say, to ask, but she manages to bite her tongue and hold them all in. Lucy is dealing with enough, and a forty'ish-year-old secret can wait another day to be answered.

Her mother was so sure she'd already met Lucas by now. Why?

The idea of who Lucas is, or who he isn't, feels a little overwhelming. Her heart flutters in her chest as she thinks about the fact that her mother expects to meet the man who is her grandfather.

How? When? Does he know she's here? Does he want to meet her? Does he care about her at all?

So many questions floating in her brain, but now is not the time for those answers.

The train station in Bruges sits outside the city core. You can reach the main square in fifteen to twenty minutes if you walk. They end up in two taxi cabs, and they take what seems to Mara, the long way around.

Mara shares a taxi with both Lucy and Jo-Jo. Jo-Jo is focused on the sites while Lucy stares straight ahead, her grip tight on her purse. Her knuckles are almost white from the strain.

"Why would Mom force you to return home?" Mara asks Lucy, keeping her voice low.

Lucy sighs and pats Mara's leg. "Stella always thought she knew best, even when she didn't. I assume she's trying to heal the past. I'd say bravo, except she took the coward's way and waited till she was gone."

"Did your family respond to your text? Did they know you were coming?"

Lucy nods. "No, no word yet, but they knew. They knew as soon as Stephanie gave them all our names for the rooms, they would have known. Now it all makes sense. Mara, there's something I need to tell you..."

"What's that?" Mara asks. From Lucy's tone, Mara knows it's not going to be good news. A weight settles deep in her stomach and she feels like she's about to be sick.

"Oh look, do you see the windmills?" Jo-Jo's voice is bright and bubbly, a complete contrast to the vibe in the taxicab and also stopping Lucy from saying anything further.

"Up on the ramparts, do you see them?" Their cab driver points out the window. Windmills? In Bruges? Sure enough, there they are, up on little hills.

"Bruges and windmills go back to the sixteenth century," their driver continues. "We used to have twenty-three of them, but now we just have the four. All but one was relocated here. That one there..." he points to the only one that seems to be moving with the wind, "still works, did you know? There's a museum, you should go and look. Bruges isn't all about chocolate and canals." The man looks at them through the mirror with a wide smile. "My family, we used to have our own, way back when. Now, now we cater to visitors like you."

Lucy looks out the window.

"She's not a visitor. This is home for her," Jo-Jo says. Either she's not reading the room, or she's ignoring the heaviness existing between Mara and Lucy right now.

"Ja?" The man rattles off sentences that Mara can't understand, and Lucy replies. He smiles at her, Lucy smiles back, then returns her attention to the window.

"He asked why we were headed to a B&B instead of my family home," Lucy explains.

"What did you say?"

"I told him to mind his own business." Lucy gives the man a half smile.

They make their way through the streets, driving down narrow roads, passing restaurants and shops that Mara knows she wants to visit, until they make a turn, and the cab driver stops at a street that resembles a driveway more than an actual road.

Mara looks around but doesn't see any signage announcing their location.

"We're here," Lucy says as she hands the driver some cash and gets out of the car.

"Where is here, exactly?" Mara glances down the street, which almost looks like a paved back alley from home.

"It's just down there," Lucy points as she waits for the trunk of the car to open.

The other car joins them, and as a group, they drag their luggage down the cobbled street.

Mara notices Lucy's steps slow the closer they get to the door.

She gives her friend a worried look. "Lucy?"

It takes a second too long for Lucy to respond. "It's just up ahead," she finally says. "We're in the guest house, and you'll need a code for the door, because, of course, no one is here to greet us."

"I've got the code," Kat says as she pulls out her phone. "Here, seven, eight, two, nine. That should unlock it."

They pass by a few windows with an etching of Barabas Bed & Breakfast in thick gold font filling the glass. Mara glances in, but between the shadows and the lack of light in the rooms within, she can only make out a table and a huge fireplace mantle.

Lucy has all but stopped in her tracks, like she's lost in a dream.

"Are you okay?" Mara asks, leaving her bag in the middle of the alleyway and returning to where Lucy has stopped. When she goes and touches her friend's hand, it's as cold as ice.

"I'm okay," Lucy finally says. "I'm just an old woman with ghosts. Come on, let's get inside." She shakes her hands as if forcing whatever is affecting her off her body, and marches to the front door, entering the code herself.

As soon as Kat opens the door, Mara sees a long staircase leading upstairs.

A long and winding staircase. She hears the muffled groans from the rest of the group, and once again, Mara's thankful not to have brought her larger suitcase.

Off to the left is a cozy room decorated in shades of brown and cream, where a few sitting chairs and a table can be seen. "The keys to our rooms should be on the table. Apparently, we're the only ones in this wing." Lucy steps into the room and inhales a long breath of air. "It...just wow," she mumbles.

"What's with all the bears?" From the decorative wood panels to embroidered wall hangings to the antique plates covering the walls, it's evident the owner of the bed and breakfast had a thing for the animals. "Please don't tell me there's a mounted bear head in our bedroom?" Mara can't imagine waking up to that every day.

"How should I know?" She circles in place, taking in everything. "Sorry, I'm just...it all looks the same and yet, so different. About the bears, there's an old medieval legend about them and Bruges. Maybe I'll tell you all tomorrow," Lucy says as she picks up keys from the table along with a printed pamphlet.

One by one, the women group off, finding their keys and trudging up the stairs with their suitcases.

"Do you want to go find your family or..." Mara asks once they're alone downstairs.

Lucy shakes her head. "If they can't be bothered to be here and greet me, then no."

Mara tries to place herself in Lucy's shoes. How would she feel if, after all these years, her family weren't here to greet her and welcome her home?

She can't imagine it, to be honest.

Lucy goes to grab her suitcase, but Mara beats her to it. "Take your time," she tells her as she heads up their narrow stairs. Navigating the stairs with two suitcases plus a large bag and purse, isn't easy, but with a little huffing, she makes it to the top, where she waits for Lucy to join her.

Her friend moves slow, and if there's ever been a time that Lucy shows her age, it's right now as she anchors one hand on the wall before taking a step.

"Do you need help?" Mara asks, concerned that maybe this is all too much for Lucy.

"I'm fine." The snarkiness doesn't go unnoticed, but Mara doesn't comment on it.

Once they open the door, a smile grows along Mara's face, and a bubble of excitement builds within her.

"This is a huge room," Mara says as she sets their luggage off to the side and then falls backward onto the bed, with her arms outstretched. "And this bed, I mean...it's like sleeping on a cloud." It doesn't even compare to what they slept on in Amsterdam.

Everything about the room suggests history and offers a sense of peace.

"This is like two hotel rooms in one," Mara continues, ignoring the fact Lucy seems speechless. "That bathroom, too," Mara twists her body around on the bed and points to the bathtub, "I bet that would fit two people," she says with a small laugh. "I might just need to kick you out of the room so I can have a nice long soak," she teases until she realizes this isn't the moment for levity.

Lucy's come home, and it seems like no one cares. That has to hurt.

"It's extravagant, and he's losing money with a room like this," Lucy mumbles. "If he were smart, he'd have converted it into a two-bedroom. It's not like him to throw money away," she continues as she steps toward one of the windows and pulls the curtain aside.

Mara doesn't ask who she's referring to. She assumes Lucy is talking about her father.

The sunlight coming into the room calls to Mara. She joins Lucy and glances out at the gorgeous backyard.

The building is a square shape with a small garden, sitting area, and a fountain, right in the middle. It's framed with a rock wall, and beyond that is one of the canals Bruges is so famous for.

Right then, a boat full of tourists slowly goes by, and someone sees them standing in the window and offers a wave.

Lucy immediately steps out of view, but Mara waves back, a wide smile on her face.

"Okay, we're doing that," she says as she looks over her shoulder. "It's like a little Venice, don't you think?" Her voice trails off as she notices the way Lucy seems to slump over as she sits down on her bed.

"Why don't you have a little nap?" Mara gently suggests. "I'm not tired anymore and would like to stretch my legs a little. I'll see if anyone else wants to join."

Lucy gives her a soft smile as she kicks off her shoes and then lies down, arranging a throw blanket around her. "That's a wonderful idea. Head back to where the driver dropped us off, turn right, take a left on the street, and follow that down until you see a small square with some restaurants. There will probably be a huge Christmas tree there with some market stalls. If you keep going, you'll find both a Christmas store and a chocolate shop and then eventually the main square. You won't get lost, and you can always use the map app on your phone to find your way back."

Mara sends a text in the group chat, and Sandra offers to join her. The rest are all going to nap. She tells Sandra she'll meet her outside and grabs her purse. When she opens the door, there's a car idling right outside, and two men stand there talking.

Not meaning to eavesdrop, she gives them both a smile and goes to walk past them, but a voice calls out to her.

"Miss? Is everything okay?"

Mara turns toward the gentleman wearing rugged jeans, a white t-shirt, and a sweater vest.

"Yes, everything is perfect, thank you," she says.

"I wasn't aware you had checked in already. I just arrived from running errands," he says, his tone sounding like an apology.

"No worries. We all found our rooms okay." Mara looks at the man. He's too young to be Lucy's father, and she never mentioned having a brother.

"And the others?"

"Most everyone is resting before dinner. I'm going to go stretch my legs before dinner," she says, feeling the need to explain herself.

The man nods. "Please, if you need anything, you let me know. There should be a card in your room with my info."

Mara gives him a smile. "Yes, of course, thank you."

There's this need to say more, but she's at a loss, and besides, it's not her place to bring up Lucy or hunt for information.

She struggles with finding words, but it turns out no words are needed. The man, still unnamed, holds the door open for Sandra, then waves before closing it behind him.

Chapter Nineteen

"I bet the town looks like it's straight from a fairytale at night with the lights," Sandra says as they sit at a cafe and stare at a gorgeous Christmas tree set up in the middle of Burg Square.

The square is lined with shops on two sides, an ornate city hall on another, and then green space. With the Christmas tree in the middle and lights strung along the buildings, sitting here, sipping a hot drink is this side of heaven.

"I'm glad you suggested doing this," Mara tells Sandra. "The others are going to regret that nap, I bet."

"I can't believe we stopped ourselves from visiting the main market." Sandra uses a spoon to finish up the last of her mocha.

"Well, it's not like we're going back empty-handed," Mara glances down at the bags at both their feet.

Slightly past this square is a side street full of chocolate, lace, and even a Christmas shop. The buildings are straight-up medieval and exactly what you'd picture in an old town like Bruges.

"We've only barely seen the town, but I can see why people love coming here. Can you imagine what it would be like in the spring and summer?" Sandra glances around and then checks her phone.

"We should head back, I guess. Everyone is up and ready for dinner."

The walk back is only about five minutes. Mara nudges the door open with her hip and immediately gets hit with a waft of freshly baked bread.

"Wow, that smells delicious." Despite the many chocolate tastings they enjoyed, her stomach rumbles for real food.

"Hello?" The man from earlier calls out, and Mara turns to find him standing behind her in the doorway.

"Just us, back from shopping," she says, holding up the bags as proof. Sandra gives a smile before she climbs the stairs.

"Ahh, you found our Christmas shop," he says, pointing to the Kathe Wohlfahrt bag. "What did you think?"

"It's the cutest store with so many things. I couldn't pass up grabbing a few nutcrackers as gifts for friends, plus a few black sheep for me." She glances inside the bag with a smile.

"Black sheep?"

Mara shrugs. "I saw them once as a teenager in Scotland and fell in love with them. They're hard to find, though. Some people collect teapots. I collect black sheep."

"Ahh," he says with a smile. "Like I collect books, and my father collects bears."

Mara nods.

"Can I interest you in some fresh tea and bread?" Without waiting for an answer, he walks through the house, leading toward the kitchen.

Mara can't help but follow. Even if she'd wanted to run upstairs to check in on Lucy and drop her bags, it can wait. Maybe she'll find out who this man is and if he's related to Lucy.

During their walk, she couldn't keep the woman out of her thoughts. She'd sent her a few messages but with no reply, assumed she was still napping. Has she spoken to her family yet? Mara couldn't imagine what Lucy must be feeling right now.

She follows him to the very homey kitchen. A large, whitewashed table fills one section of the room, with a cozy kitchen on the other. Propped on the island are fresh loaves of bread.

"Please, have a seat."

Mara places a hand on a chair, but she can't help but take everything in.

"I'm sure you hear this all the time, but your home is amazing," Mara can barely withhold the marvel in her voice.

There's something about this room that speaks family. Maybe it's the photos on the walls. Maybe it's the children's drawings on the fridge. Maybe it's the height markers found in the doorway, or maybe, just maybe, it's the whole vibe of the home.

"I agree," he says. "I don't think I've introduced myself. I'm Bram, and this has been our family home for almost twelve generations now. On that door behind you, in blue, that's me." He points toward a little stick figure drawn in blue marker, now faded.

Mara can't help but smile. She notices there's also a figure in green and in pink. "Your siblings?" Is he Lucy's brother, then?

Bram smiles. "Yes. One is gone, the other…well, I've been waiting for her to come back home."

That confirms it. It's on the tip of her tongue to mention Lucy, to say something about her, but she stops herself. It's not her place to speak for Lucy, and as Stella would say, it's not her story. Looking at him, she can kind of see the resemblance in both the eyes and smile.

"I'm so sorry," Mara says. "Losing family is difficult. My mother recently passed away," she says softly as she finds herself walking toward a kitchen cabinet covered in family photos.

"I'm sorry for your loss," Bram says, with a slight catch in his voice.

Mara glances at him, and she sees genuine sadness.

"Thank you," because what else would she say? "My mother had dementia, so while I mourn, I'm also…" she can't find the right words. She's not happy her mother is gone, she will never be happy or glad or even relieved. But she is…

"At peace, maybe? Knowing her suffering is done?"

Mara nods. Yes, that's exactly how she's feeling. At peace.

"I hope you don't feel guilty for feeling that way. I doubt your mother would want you to feel one ounce of shame or guilt for moving on with your life."

Mara heads back to the table and pulls out the chair. "No, she wouldn't. In fact, she's the one who insisted I join my friends on this trip. We travel yearly over the holidays and love to explore the Christmas Markets. This is our first time in Belgium, though. In fact, it was my mom who told us about this place." Mara says, trying hard not to say too much, not to mention Lucy.

Bram pulls out a knife from a drawer, not looking at her. "Would you like coffee or tea?"

"Coffee, please," she says. She keeps an eye on him, waiting for a reaction, but he gives her none.

Instead, he turns his back and makes her a coffee from his espresso machine. Once that is done, he brings over a platter with freshly sliced bread, what looks like homemade jam, and coffee.

Mara notices how he won't look her in the eye, and it makes her wonder if he's nervous about seeing Lucy after all this time.

"I mentioned it was my mother who suggested we stay here..." Why is she repeating herself? Now, he's going to realize Lucy's return wasn't intentional.

"Your mother? And her name was..."

"Stella Pearce."

Bram heads back into the kitchen, but she catches the slight falter in his steps.

"Mara?"

She turns as she hears Lucy's voice calling to her.

"In here, Lucy."

There's a loud shatter of what sounds like glass breaking, and she glances over to find Bram dropping out of sight.

She gets up and rushes over, worried something is wrong. She finds him on his knees, cleaning up the broken glass. "Are you okay?" She notices drops of blood dripping on the floor.

"Mara?"

She gets to her feet and grabs a cloth from the counter, handing it to Bram.

"How was your rest?" Mara asks Lucy, noticing an increased tension in the room.

"It was fine. Everyone is ready to head out for dinner, and I thought you might want to freshen up a little before we do. What's going on here?"

Mara waits for Bram to say something, but he won't even look up, solely focused on cleaning the glass, picking up each piece individually.

"Lucy, this is...um...Bram." She feels so stupid for the introduction since, of course, they would know each other. "I think he nicked his hand on some broken glass. Do you have a broom and duster handy?" She asks, looking around but seeing no cleaning objects.

Lucy heads over to a cabinet off to the side, opens the door, and pulls one out. "Not much around here has changed, has it?" She joins Bram and starts sweeping up the mess, almost forcing Bram out of the way.

"You need a bandage on that." Lucy's tone is gruff, almost to the point of harsh.

"I'm fine." Bram's lips knit together in stubbornness.

"You're not fine. If you were, you wouldn't be bleeding all over the place." She grabs a cloth hanging from a cupboard drawer, wets it in the sink, and then drops it on the floor, using her foot to clean it up.

"You haven't changed, have you?" Bram mutters.

"Neither have you, apparently." Lucy's lips quirk as she sneaks a glance toward Mara.

There's a feeling of familiarity between the two, and Mara has a hard time believing they've been estranged for all this time. What happened that Lucy would disassociate herself from her family?

"This was not how I thought this family reunion would go," Bram says as he places a bandaid on his hand. He heads to a closet and pulls out a bottle. "I think this calls for a wee nib, don't you?" He gathers three small espresso cups in one hand, the bottle of liquor in the other, and plops them down on the table. "Sit, both of you." He orders.

Lucy takes one seat, Mara the other.

No one says a word while Bram pours a large splash of the golden amber into the cups.

Bram clears his throat as he raises his glass. "I think a toast is in order. To family...old," he glances toward Lucy, "and new," he says, looking at Mara.

Mara's brown furrows. To family? Old and new?

"Welcome home, sister," Bram continues. "And to you, Mara, it's nice to meet my niece, finally."

Chapter Twenty

Going out with the others to sit in a restaurant and stew over the news is not what Mara wants to do right this minute, and yet, somehow, she finds herself being pulled along despite telling everyone she needed some alone time and would meet them later.

What she really needs is a break from Lucy. That, or a simple, honest talk where the woman stops withholding things from her.

For some reason, she has a hard time believing that will happen. If Lucy hadn't been honest before now, why would that change after what happened in the kitchen?

First - they're related.

Second - they're related, and Lucy has never said anything.

Third - she's her aunt and even her mother kept this a secret!

Fourth - she has family that has never reached out. How is she supposed to feel about that or even deal with it? Especially since she's basically staying in their home, where seeing each other is unavoidable.

What she's struggling with, though is how both her mother and Lucy could keep this a secret for so long. This feels like something Mara should have known, right from the beginning.

Mara's grip on her crossbody purse tightens, and she has to

remind herself to relax. The last thing she needs is for the rest of the group to pick up on what's going on between her and Lucy.

She's doing a piss-poor job at hiding it if the questioning looks from the others is any indication. Lucy's as silent as she is, and even though they've been paired up as they walk through the streets, Mara refuses to look at Lucy. One glance is all it will take for Mara to lose it, and that's the last thing she wants to do right now.

Kat had suggested they go on a walking tour and visit the main market, but everyone else was hungry, and the thought of enjoying the markets at night, with all the lights twinkling, won in the end.

Once they make it to Au Petit Grand, Sandra waits until everyone else has entered the restaurant before stopping Mara and Lucy.

"I know something happened between you two, the miserable emotions coming off you both are ridiculous. I don't know what's going on, but can you have a nice dinner with us all, or do you need to deal with," she waves her hands between them, "whatever this is, first?"

Mara raises her brow to Lucy, indicating the decision is hers.

The firmness in Lucy's lips is all the answer she needs.

"I did try to warn you guys when I said I needed time alone." Mara reminds her.

"Regardless, that doesn't answer my question," Sandra says.

Mara looks at Lucy once again. "We will be fine," she tells Sandra. "You're right, something is going on between us, but we can be adults about it, can't we?" She directs this to Lucy with a hint of frostiness.

Lucy gives a slight nod, and that is all Sandra needs. She makes them sit on opposite sides, like children, but Mara can't blame her. To the unknown, they probably look like they're acting like children.

What will they say when they find out the truth?

After a meal of what might as well have been porridge and burnt toast for Mara, they head toward the Grote Markt, the main square in central Bruges, and they all stand there for a few minutes to take it all in.

Mara's sullenness dissipates as she takes in her surroundings as if by magic and she'll take it. Ignoring the chaotic whirlwind threatening to toss her about for an hour or two sounds is exactly what she needs.

"It's exactly like the photos you always see online," Jo-Jo says in an awe-inspired voice. "The tall multicolored brick buildings, the pointed gingerbread roofs, the lights...that's it, I'm coming back here in the summer to see the square naked and in its true form."

"It's perfect, just as it is," Kat says with an absolute smile. "This is what a square should be like, don't you think? The main commerce area for towns like this. Imagine what it was like back then." She pulls out her camera. "I love how the towering Belfry, the Provincial Palace, and the guild houses all frame the market. With the cobblestone streets, gingerbread huts edged in lights...it's just simply...perfect."

"I think perfect is your new favorite word." Donna too pulls out her phone and starts taking photos. "Brrr. I should have brought my mitts." She quickly replaces her phone in her purse and hides her hands in her jacket pockets. "I swear it's gotten colder since we left the restaurant."

"Honey, it is the beginning of December. There may not be snow, but that doesn't mean it's not going to get cold." Sandra hands Donna one of the extra mitts she keeps in her bag. "These should help. You should look for some handmade ones here, I'm sure there will be a vendor selling alpaca gloves."

Mara pulls out her handmade red gloves with the maple leaf stitched onto them, a gift from Gus and Lily, well, Lily since she made them.

"You know, that's the one thing I wish for when we come to these. The snow. That would add to the magic, don't you think?" Mara buttons up the top of her coat.

"I'm okay without it, *thank-you-very-much*," Lucy mutters. "We get enough of it at home."

Mara nods in agreement before she remembers she's upset with the woman.

Sandra notices the quick tightening of Mara's lips and rolls her eyes. "All right, ladies, I'm ready to shop. Let's do our usual, shall we? See that restaurant over there on the corner? If we separate, that will be our meeting stop where we can have one last drink of something warm before we head back to the B&B, okay?"

The crowded square makes it hard for everyone to stay together. Some pair up, while others go on their own. Mara finds herself sticking close to Lucy, whether out of habit or to keep an eye on the older woman, or so that she doesn't feel so alone…she's not sure, nor is she willing to delve deep into the reasoning. Despite that, she keeps Lucy in her sights while leaving a bit of distance between them.

There are a few things Mara looks for at every market. The main one is a vendor selling gluwein. While she enjoys the mulled wine, she is especially interested in the souvenir mug found at most markets. She tries to make it a goal to keep one mug from every market they visit and showcase them on the wall back home. She's been spying on the mugs everyone holds and knows she has to have one. She sees both red and white cups with an image of Santa Claus flying over the steeped roofs of the medieval houses, pulled by the swans Bruges is known for.

"Stella would have loved these." Lucy appears beside her with her own mug in hand.

Mara can only nod. She was thinking the same thing.

She feels torn. Torn between wanting and needing to be angry with Stella for keeping this secret, and the need to remember her mom as she once was, while she was still healthy. She loved the markets, loved coming on these trips. Mara doesn't want to ruin that memory with all the revelations.

She also knows, that instead of being honest with that anger and directing it toward someone who isn't here, she's placing it all on Lucy, which, while understandable, isn't fair to the older woman.

She kept all of this a secret, sure, but she's not the only one responsible. Mara needs to remember that.

"She'd also be in line for one of those waffles," Mara says, doing her best to place all those emotions and thoughts into their own little box. "Mom would always eat a light meal and skip dessert to try all the local foods." Her mother had been a small woman with a high metabolism, something Mara did not inherit from her.

"I'm ready to talk," Lucy says after they walk down a pathway together.

"So am I." Mara would love to shop, but her heart isn't in it. How can it be? Ever since her mom's death, she's been trying to deal with being alone, truly alone with no family, only to find out that's not true. She's had family surrounding her all along, and while that fills a part of the hole in her spirit, it also fills her with anger and a sense of betrayal.

She's so tired of being in the dark and hates the confusion circling inside her right now.

They find a table beneath a heat lamp at the restaurant where they are to meet everyone at, and both order a hot toddy. "I'll need a few sips before we get into this," Lucy cautions Mara.

"Well, your secret has waited this long, hasn't it?" The bite in her tone doesn't go unnoticed by how Lucy winces.

She's always known there was more to the woman than she knew, but she never imagined this.

She somehow manages to wait while Lucy enjoys her drink before the questions start flowing.

"My aunt? How can you be family and never tell me? Especially with us coming here? Did my mom know? Of course, she knew, that was a stupid question." Mara rubs her hands together. "How could you both keep this a secret from me? Why? Is there something so horrible with your family that you wouldn't tell me?" Tears well up as the words blubber from her mouth. She grabs the napkin to dab the tears away, but they keep coming.

Lucy reaches out a hand and grabs Mara.

"I wanted to tell you from the moment we first met in Paris," she says softly, her voice wobbly with emotion. "Keeping this secret from you has been the hardest thing I've ever done. But I've always told you we were family."

Mara snorts. "Yeah, but not by blood, just by love."

"Is there a difference?"

Mara yanks her hand away. "Of course, there's a difference. Who doesn't want a family?" She leans back in her chair and looks out over the crowds. "Oh, I know Mom always said we were the only family we ever needed and that we create the family we want, but that's not the same, and you know it."

"You're right, and I'm sorry," Lucy says, her voice catching. "I'm so, so sorry."

Mara waits a moment to let the apology sink in. Is it enough? Can words of contrition ease all the hurt?

"I don't want your sorries," she finally says, letting her truth speak for itself. "I want answers, Lucy. Or do I call you Aunt Lucy now?" She wraps her bare hands around the warm mug, her tears dried up. "Crap, Lucy...how could you?"

"I wanted to respect your mother's wishes, Mara."

Mara almost didn't hear the words; they were so soft.

"That's just an excuse." Somehow, Mara finds the strength to hold onto how she's feeling, rather than giving in and providing Lucy an easy out.

There are a few ways she can deal with this. She can do the polite thing, the thing that comes so easy to her, and forgive Lucy, say she understands, think about the pain Lucy must be in right now being forced to return home, and put her own feelings to the side.

She can listen and try to understand Lucy's explanation.

Or she can be selfish and let this be all about her, how she's the one who's been wronged, how she's the one who's been left in the dark, lied to her whole life. She can let this be all about her and demand answers.

Except, that's not really her.

She decided to go with her heart and speak freely and honestly, letting the words and emotions come as they will. She trusts Lucy. Despite everything, Lucy has been a constant in her life, and she knows that won't change.

"I thought I was doing the right thing in keeping your mom's secret, Mara." Lucy leans forward, elbows on the table, and Mara reads the truth in her eyes.

"She was wrong, and you and I both know it."

"You're right," Lucy nods. "I'll keep saying it because it's the truth: I'm sorry. It is an excuse, but it's also the truth. You know what your mother was like. Stubborn as all get out."

Mara takes a sip of the delicious butterscotch-tasting drink. "I don't know who I'm more angry at, you or her."

"That's legit. Will you let me explain, please?"

Mara nods.

"That Paris trip was a complete fluke. I had no idea, I swear, that either you or your mother would be there. How much do you remember from when we first met?"

Mara thinks back to when Lucy entered their lives. That Paris trip was a spur-of-the-moment, let's do what we've always talked about doing, and when they saw that one of their favorite authors was hosting a reader trip to Europe, they booked right away. A sweet tour in Paris, how could they pass that up? It was a small group tour where they bonded with a few of the other women who came. She remembers how happy she was that her mom found not just one friend but also a group of friends that became more than just travel companions.

"You and Mom seemed to partner off together a lot. You'd go for coffee during downtime, you'd chat and laugh, and it was like you both had an instant connection. But I guess it wasn't so instant, was it?"

"No, it wasn't. It was, however a surprise to see her, and you. It was the turning point for my life."

Mara frowned. "Turning point?"

Lucy sighs. "I left my family for you."

She what? "That doesn't make sense."

"When your mother left here," Lucy waves her hand around, "that was the last anyone heard from her. She was gone, out of our lives, out of my life. No one knew about you; at least, I didn't. So, when I first met her in Paris, it was like seeing a ghost."

Something shudders across her face.

"It took her a long time to introduce us. Do you remember that? That first day at the hotel when we were all checking in, you probably don't remember me, it was so chaotic. We both arrived at the same time. I think you went to your room with all your luggage while your mom stayed behind."

Mara nods. "That was normal, though. Mom always liked to sit down in the lounge of whatever hotel we were staying at and people watch. She'd sip coffee and stay there till I came down. She had a thing about not being in the hotel room until it was time for bed on our first days."

"Probably because of the bed," Lucy says with a chuckle. "It's so tempting to take a short nap, even though that's the worst thing you can do when you travel overseas. Stella used to tell me she had no self-control when napping after a long flight, so she'd rather stay in the lounge and drink coffee while you got everything settled in the room."

"I had no idea you were her daughter until everyone introduced themselves at the dinner. And even then, I didn't clue in that we were family until later when you mentioned your age."

"Honestly?" Why Mara finds that hard to believe, she's not sure. Stella was stubborn, and it isn't surprising that she'd been kept a secret.

"Honey," Lucy reaches for Mara's hand, "your mother had an instant, all-encompassing love affair with my younger brother and then disappeared."

This is the first mention of Mara's father, and Mara isn't about to let this moment go.

"Tell me about him."

"Jules...he was...the baby."

"Jules? That's his name?"

"Julien. I called him Jules."

Was. Called. That says everything.

"So, Lucas is your father, Bram, your brother, and then Jules." His name on her tongue felt foreign.

"From Mom's letters, she makes it sound like he's alive."

"I wish he were. Your mother knew we had so many talks about him and his passing, so I'm sorry she didn't share that in her letters. I can only think that in her heart, she still believed him to be here."

"So he was the youngest? How much younger than you?" She wants to know everything about him.

"It was Bram, me, and Jules. He was a few years older than your mom, and a few years younger than me. Oh honey, if he'd known about you...he would have moved heaven and earth to be in your life."

"But he did. Mom said he knew, and he still chose your family."

Lucy played with the cup she held, turning it in circles on the table. "I know what your mother believed. This was something Stella and I disagreed on."

"What did..." she struggles with calling him dad, or even father. He wasn't either of those things to her just like she's struggling with calling Lucy, Aunt. "What did Julien have to say? Mom tended to dig her heels in when it came to her stubbornness, but..." she hesitates before asking the one question she needs to know. "Did he know about me?"

Sadness wraps around Lucy like a heavy winter coat. "Eventually." She bit her lip like she's struggling not to say more. "Listen, Mara, my brother...he was as stubborn as your mother, and he tended to close himself off when hurt. When your mom left, out of the blue with no warning...he changed into someone I didn't recognize, and we started to grow apart."

"Mom broke his heart." Her letters make it sound like her heart was broken, too.

Lucy pulls an envelope from her purse and slides it across the table. "I think it's time for this next letter. Your mother...was vivacious and irresistible; there was something about her back then that burned bright, and everyone in her sphere couldn't help but want more of her. We had no choice. I'm not sure if she understood her allure back then."

Mom was always larger than life. She was Mara's everything and sometimes overshadowed everyone else in her life, so she understands that.

Mara lets it sink in - that Mom never told Julien about her. She still can't fathom how she's supposed to feel about that. Angry? Sad? Resigned?

It just is what it is. That's the emotion. That's the vibe. It is what it is.

Chapter Twenty-One

Dear Mara-mine,

Let's talk about Lucy. I hope she doesn't read this letter, but if she does, because she's too nosey to respect your privacy, then that's on her.

You should know by now that Lucy is family. She's your aunt. You're only aunt. Even without that title, she's always been family for us.

I love Lucy like a sister, I always have, right from the moment I first met her.

Has she told you about that yet?

I was a girl on her own in a beautiful town, but sometimes I felt alone. I'd met your father, but he had his job, and responsibilities, so often I'd be on my own, especially in the evenings.

Lucy rescued me one night and dragged me to this tiny little bar that was down an alley, unknown to the tourists. I don't remember the name, but I do remember that it had a red door against a white brick building with a sign that it started in 1515. (I asked Lucy, and she said it's called Lissinghe, and it's the oldest bar in Bruges).

I know you're probably upset with her. Probably not as mad at her as you are at me, but, know that I asked her to keep my secret - and she didn't want to.

You probably want to know why. You've probably already asked Lucy why, and she only told you that it was my decision.

I figure you deserve to hear about why from me.

Mara, I'm a stubborn woman. You know that about your mom. Stubborn to a fault, whether it's right or not. You got that, honestly, at least.

I made a vow to walk away from that family, and I was determined to keep it.

As much as I loved Lucy as a young girl, she was/is still part of that family that broke my heart, and I have never been able to forgive them.

When I saw Lucy in Paris, I wanted to run. I wanted to grab you and make some pithy excuse about leaving the tour group and doing Paris on our own, and I almost did.

Almost.

Lucy convinced me otherwise.

At first, she had no clue you even existed. She didn't even know to ask about you. There was the excitement and instant connection that existed between us - and the years apart melted away. I'll be honest, they even melted away a bit of the anger I held toward her.

It took her a few days to gather the nerve to ask me if you were her niece. I wanted to lie, and I almost did. It would have been so easy to pass you off as another man's child. I was young and full of life, who's to say I didn't meet someone else after I left Belgium?

I couldn't do that, though. Not after I saw the connection between you and her. Do you remember what you said to me after the first day meeting her? 'She's someone I need in my life, like she's a part of me'.

I couldn't do that to you.

So I told her if she wanted to be part of your life, she needed to keep my secret. I didn't ask. I didn't beg, either. That was my condition. All I wanted was to protect you.

She's kept my secret for all these years, simply out of love. Love for you. Love for me. Especially once she found out the truth.

So don't be angry with her. This was my decision. Looking back, I wouldn't have done anything differently, and I hope you can understand that.

I love you.
Mom

Chapter Twenty-Two

While Mara reads the letter, the rest of their group joins them at the table. Mara slides the envelope into her bag, struggling to process even more news, and looks at Lucy, silently asking if she wants this shared with the others.

Lucy only shrugs. What kind of answer is that?

"Looks like you two made up," Sandra says, sitting beside Mara. "Good. Families all have their quibbles, but in the end, the bond between the two of you is stronger than any argument."

Mara wonders if Sandra knows the truth or if maybe she has an inkling. It wouldn't surprise her if Stella talked to her. Sandra probably knows more secrets within this group than anyone else.

They spend the next half hour sipping hot drinks while sharing their purchases and Jo-Jo scrolling through all the photos she took. By the time they walk back to the B&B, they're not only talked out, but everyone seems ready for bed.

Mara realizes, following their conversation, that she has yet to ask about Lucas, Lucy's father. Thinking that's something to discuss back in the room, she realizes talking is the last thing Lucy wants to do as she watches her friend wearily climb the stairs.

The stairs of her childhood home. The stairs of Mara's family home.

That feels so weird to think about. This is the home of her family. Distant, almost non-existent family, but a family nonetheless.

That in itself feels weird to think about. She has family. She's not alone, not anymore.

No family is perfect, Mara knows that. Just listening to the others talk about issues they're all having, it proves that. And this family, Lucy's family, is full of secrets. One after the other, never-ending, always growing...it almost makes Mara thankful she hasn't been part of it.

Until now.

Even with the messiness, sitting at the table with Bram and Lucy, feeling the connectedness between them, even if it was tense, gave her a sense of what she'd been missing all these years.

Life is messy. Family, especially so. Regardless of what it meant to have this family in her life, there's a part of her that realizes she missed out.

Mara heads to the kitchen for some water, and while pouring it from the waiting jug resting on the counter, Bram appears in the doorway, his hair slightly messy, like he'd been running his fingers through it.

"How was dinner and the market?" He asks.

"Confusing," Lucy says, deciding to go with honesty over politeness.

"So you talked?" He heads toward the fridge and pulls out a glass jug of what looks to be homemade iced tea.

He pours a little into a cup, takes a sip, and then fishes out the teabags drowning in the liquid. "I made this earlier after you left. Would you like some? It used to be Lucy's favorite."

Mara can't help but smile at the fact he made the drink just for Lucy.

"Maybe a little. Caffeine and me don't get along too well at bedtime." She watches as he pours a little into the glass. "Lucy's still as addicted to the stuff. She used to tell me her mother would keep a jug sitting on the windowsill so it could get kissed by the sun."

The smile on Bram's face is bittersweet. "Mom used to do that when we were kids," he said.

Over the years, Lucy had told her so many stories of her childhood. It's too bad she never clued into the truth of why Lucy would share these little hints of her past.

"I was a young man when our mother died, but it hit Lucy the most, I think. A lot of the household chores settled on her shoulders, even though we all pitched in as best we could. Even when Dad turned this place into a B&B, hiring Shari to help run the day-to-day, Lucy still took on way too much." He brought over two glasses, glancing through the doorway with a slight hesitation.

"She headed up to the room. Said she needed a nice long soak in the tub and then sleep."

He nods as if understanding, but she catches the shard of disappointment on his face.

"I bet you have a lot of questions, and knowing my sister, I doubt she answered much of them. I won't be able to either, but I can try," he says.

Questions? She has so many, to the point where it's almost debilitating. Where does she even start? And who's story does she want told the most? Her father's? Her mother's?

"Where is Lucas?"

Bram leans back in his seat and frowns.

"In bed. He...well, he isn't well." He says this with a note of finality.

"I'm sorry."

He nods. "Knowing Lucy is here but that she hasn't been to see him, it wore him out. My father is a stubborn man and has refused all treatment, so it's just a matter of time."

"Waiting for him to die." She says this not as a question but with sympathy, speaking as one who knows exactly what it means to wait for someone to pass away.

"When he found out Lucy was coming back, it seemed to rally him. Maybe tomorrow..." he doesn't finish his sentence, as if realizing how useless it is to suggest Lucy will act in any way but her own.

"She can be stubborn," Mara admits. "I only found out that she grew up here a few days ago. As far as I knew, she didn't have any living family left."

It was like she stuck him with a knife.

"She said that? That we were dead?"

Mara shakes her head, realizing the need to correct her words. "I think it was more that she didn't have any family left, so I assumed she meant everyone had died."

He nods as if understanding. "The last time I saw her was when she stormed out the front door. She told my father we were dead to her, and that was that. Never heard another word until I got the reservation."

Lucy and Stella were more alike than either one of them wanted to admit. Mara's always known this, but Bram's words solidify the knowledge.

"Did she tell you why?" He seems hesitant.

Mara shakes her head. "I don't expect you to tell me either. That is her story to tell. When she's ready."

He looks down at the cup in his hands, as if he should be able to find the answers to all his questions in his cold tea.

"Do you want to meet Lucas?" He finally says as he glances up at her. "I don't...well, I don't know what Stella told you, or even my sister for that matter, and I don't want to assume."

Mara lifts a shoulder in a shrug. "Part of me does. I have so many questions that need answered and—"

"This may sound harsh, but...don't expect any answers from

him. If you want to meet him because he's family, that's one thing. If you want to meet him to get closure on a past you never knew… you will probably end up disappointed."

Disappointment is a sweater Mara has been breaking in for a long time.

"Any other advice then?"

He glances around the kitchen. "Feel free to make yourself at home. You may be able to find some answers by familiarizing yourself with the place your mother once loved." He drinks the last of his tea. "Tomorrow, after breakfast, if you have no plans, I'll show you our personal area. You'll also be able to meet Shari."

Mara remembers Lucy mentioning Shari.

"Shari still works here?"

"She lives next door, actually. She's family now. After Lucy left, I realized family is what you make it to be."

"That's what Mom always said, too. We choose our family, the ones we let into our lives and become a part of us."

"I didn't interact much with your mother. I was away at school then, but Jules called and told me all about her. In fact, if I look, I can find some of his journals that he kept around that time. I don't know what will be in them, or even if the answers you're seeking will be there, but I can look."

A tiny bubble of excitement found its way into Mara's heart.

"I would love that, thank you."

Heading back to her room, she's surprised to find Sandra sitting on the stairs, hands clasped around her knees.

"Everything okay?"

Sandra pats the space beside her on the stairs, and Mara squeezes in. It's a rather narrow area, but they manage to fit.

"I came down to see if there was some cream in the fridge for my sleep tea, and I overheard you and our host talking," Sandra admits, her voice whisper-like.

Mara doesn't know what to say. She got the impression Lucy wasn't ready to tell the girls about their connection, and in all honesty, Mara gets it. There will be many questions that Lucy won't want to answer and even some hurt feelings that a secret like this was kept from them.

She is still having a hard time with it. For all the years Lucy has been in her life, she never, never would have thought they were related. Not for real.

"Crazy, right?"

"I'm trying to put myself in your shoes. No wonder you were so upset over dinner. You probably just found out, didn't you? And here we were, dragging you out when you very clearly stated you needed time alone. I'm so sorry, Mara. For... well, for everything. For the secrets that were kept from you, for losing your Mom so close to your birthdays and the holidays, for..."

Mara places her hand on Sandra's arm and lightly squeezes. "Stop. You have nothing to apologize for. Yeah, it's a lot, and I'm not going to lie, I'm struggling to wrap my head around it all. I'm trying to remember that this isn't just about me. My mom tricked Lucy into returning home...I can't even imagine what Lucy is feeling right now."

Sandra gives her a tight side hug and doesn't let go.

"Tomorrow, I think the two of you need a day to yourselves. Kat has us on an early walk around town and then a day filled with sightseeing and shopping, but you two don't need to join us. You've got other things to deal with, okay?"

Mara nods. "That's probably a good idea. Can you...keep this between us for now? I'm sure we'll tell everyone, but..."

"Of course." Sandra gets up and holds a hand out. "I'll skip my tea tonight. We'll hook up tomorrow, okay? We'll keep you updated on where we are if you decide you want to join, but no pressure. I think this trip's focus has changed for you and Lucy. Family always comes first."

Mara lets out something between a chuckle and a snort. "Family. I don't even know what to do with that."

They slowly walk up the stairs, keeping their footsteps light on the wood floor.

"There's a story in there, that's for sure, don't you think?" Sandra asks. "I can't wait to hear all about it."

Chapter Twenty-Three

After tossing and turning all night, Mara stumbles down the stairs to the back porch area where breakfast is being served. It's a good thing she woke up when she did, otherwise she would have missed it. She can't believe Lucy let her sleep in this long.

The others left around forty minutes ago for their morning tour and her phone has been blowing up with photos Jo-Jo keeps sharing. Bruges is such a beautiful town, she almost wishes she was on the tour as well.

As she rounds the corner, a woman's laughter greets her from the kitchen, where Lucy is standing close to an older woman wearing an apron.

"Good morning, sleepy head," Lucy says, coming over to give her a hug. "I wasn't sure if you were going to sleep past breakfast or not."

"Did you turn off my alarm?"

Lucy nods. "You didn't sleep well last night, and there's no rush today. The others left and have their day already planned. Figure we can meet up with them later if we want." Lucy explains.

"Makes sense, thanks. Sorry if I kept you up with all my tossing and turning." The dark circles beneath Lucy's eyes confirm she didn't sleep well either.

"Have you had breakfast yet?"

"No, I wanted to wait for you," Lucy gives her a smile. "I've been catching up with Shari, which has been so nice."

Mara gives the woman a smile.

"Nice to finally meet you, Mara. We'll need to chat, but first, why don't you take a seat, and I'll bring everything out to you. Imagine, aunt and niece finally in this house. It's been too long."

Mara gives an awkward smile. Things still don't feel real.

"Let me grab you some coffee," Shari says as she leads the way to the dining area. "Lucy, you go sit, too." She points toward a table in the middle of the room, and both women sit as instructed.

The room itself isn't too large, it's more like a sunroom than a dining room. There are three round tables, all covered in white tablecloths, silver tier trays full of baked goods, assortments of cheese, and even a large chocolate egg. The place settings are gorgeous fine blue china that looks old and delicate. At one end of the room is a large painted mural with a breakfast bar along the wall, and the other end is a large closed-in library bookshelf, complete with books, old china teapots, and antique clocks.

"This is beautiful," Mara can't help but utter. Toward the back is a large painted angel located above a set of doors.

"Still using the family china, I'm surprised," Lucy says as she lightly touches the plate.

"Well, you get the family china, yes. Generally, we use whatever we pick up at the antique markets," Shari says as she points toward the other tables that have different china settings.

Shari heads over to the breakfast bar, where she fills a tray with dishes. She sets down bowls of fresh fruit, granola, and yogurt. "How would you like your eggs this morning? I also have bacon or ham?"

"Um, I'm more than happy with this egg right here," Mara pulls the chocolate egg off the tiered tray and places it in a small bowl, using her spoon to break it open. Chocolate at breakfast, what a wonderful idea.

"You don't have to go to so much bother for us," Lucy says. "I can also help out in the kitchen."

"And I said I didn't want your help. I've done just fine all these years without you here, *thank-you-very-much*," Shari grumbles.

"I'll take over hard with bacon, please," Mara interjects before an argument breaks out. "Lucy likes hers over easy, and you can add her bacon to my plate." She tosses a saucy grin toward Lucy, but the woman isn't paying her any attention.

Her focus is outside, past the large bay windows, overlooking the patio. There's a bevy of activity out there this morning, with five people wearing all white arranging tables and chairs.

"We have a small wedding reception happening this afternoon," Shari explains. "Fully catered, thankfully. Bram is a genius when it comes to marketing, and we are quite often booked for receptions and photos during the wedding season."

"Isn't it too cold?" Mara couldn't imagine holding a reception outdoors in December.

"We have heat lamps, plus, we'll be setting up these areas as well for the guests. The weather is beautiful today, and the bride specifically requested to be outdoors if it was nice out, so..." she shrugs as if saying 'what do you do'.

"That's a lot of pressure on you," Lucy says.

"Nonsense. My daughter handles all the bookings, and we work with local caterers to provide the food. Barabas has become quite the name," Shari says with a sense of pride. "We've even been featured in different magazines and online sites."

"What does Barabas stand for?" Mara asks, looking toward Lucy with her question.

"It's a family name," Lucy says softly, "as one of the oldest citizens of Bruges."

Mara lets that sink in for a moment. Oldest citizens of Bruges.

So, this really is home for Lucy. Not just a place where she grew up, but a place where the roots of her family go deep.

Growing up, setting roots meant staying in a place long enough to build friendships. Cochrane is home. The bookstore, her friends…those have always been her roots.

Once, in school, she had to build a family tree. Hers was pathetic, especially compared to others in her class. Her family tree has grown now, and instead of there being one branch of family members, her whole tree is probably filled out with ancestors she's never known about.

The idea of all she's missed out on is starting to sink in.

Mara points toward the large mural on the wall. "Are those family members?"

Lucy tilts her head as she stares at the painting. "Why is that familiar?"

"The tapestry," Shari says, her voice soft, as if nudging a memory into the forefront.

"Right," Lucy says. "I noticed that wasn't in the sitting room, but figured you moved it."

"We had to send it off to be restored," Shari explains. "It's so iconic though, that your father suggested we have it painted on the wall there. Guests love it and often ask questions about it. That and the fireplace seem to be the most popular items in the house."

"So where is it now?" Lucy asks.

"In the residence."

Lucy nods. "Makes sense, I guess. It's more protected there than in here, with all the guests."

"Residence?"

Shari nods and points toward the wall to their right. "It's next door. It's where Bram and Lucas live. Honestly, Lucy, I'm surprised you didn't stay there. That's home, and your room is still there. I did it up, just in case you decide you want to move over."

Something in Lucy changes. "That's not my home, not anymore. I meant what I said when I left, and you, of all people, should understand that better than anyone." Lucy pushes back her chair with enough force that it screeches against the floor.

"Where are you going?" Mara asks, not sure what's going on.

"For a walk. I'll be back in an hour. The girls are headed to a chocolate class in a few hours, do you want to go? If so, I'll see you back here and we can walk over together." She rushes out of the room, leaving Mara sitting there before she can say a word.

"That woman. Still as stubborn as the day she was born. I thought..." Shari stops herself with a shake of her head. "Never mind that now, let me get that egg started, and I'll grab your coffee."

So many questions swirl in the air, questions Mara knows she needs to ask. But who will give her an honest answer?

Did her mother understand how coming back here would affect Lucy? Did she know and not care? That doesn't sound like Stella.

Knowing her mother, Stella knew the exact cost this trip would take on Lucy. She probably hoped for some healing to occur, but that's not fair to Lucy.

Except, when it comes to Stella, Mara has always known her mother never played fair.

Chapter Twenty-Four

"Listen," Mara tries to get Lucy to slow her pace as they weave through the narrow and crooked streets of Bruges. "Honestly, Lucy, stop, please."

"We're going to be late," Lucy repeats, the only words she's spoken since returning back to the B&B.

"Just because the others are going to this class, doesn't mean we have to. At least you don't have to. Don't you want to spend time with your brother? With your father?" Who, she doesn't point out but wants to, she hasn't met yet.

The woman beside her huffs but finally slows her pace. Her chest heaves, but Mara isn't sure if it's from unexpressed emotion or from the pace she's kept since they walked out the doors.

"And what exactly am I going to do, huh? What exactly do you think is going to happen while we're here, Mara?"

There's too much anger and confrontation in Lucy's tone.

That doesn't scare her. It never has. It never will. She knows Lucy too well. Those emotions need to go someplace, and why not toward someone safe?

"Oh, I don't know," she says as she steps out of the way of a large group stealing up the sidewalk. "Maybe spend some time with your family? Reconnect? Deal with whatever it was that made you run away?"

Lucy snorts. "Run away? Is that what you think I did? Oh, that's rich."

"What else am I supposed to think? You dole out information like it's a hot commodity and make me feel like the price is too steep for me to pay." She grabs Lucy's arm and pulls her to the side.

"For you to pay? Come on, Mara, you can do better than that. You see more than you let on, you always have. Stop thinking about yourself for once. Maybe you're not the one having to pay the price for sharing my past, have you thought of that?" That admission takes all the steam out of Lucy, and she drops onto a bench. "I never wanted to return here. Never. I swore I never would. Not because I ran away, but because I was running to something. To you. To Stella. To the only family that meant anything to me. Don't you see that?"

Mara joins Lucy on the bench, realizing how fragile things are between the two of them.

"I don't, Lucy, and I'm sorry about that," she says, her voice a lot softer than before. "You're asking me to put together a puzzle that's missing all the key pieces. It's an impossible task."

"You're right." Her chest heaves as she inhales and slowly lets out all the tension. Her shoulders deflate as she stares out toward the street. "You're right, and I'm..." Lucy plays with the purse that's sitting in her lap. "I'm the coward in this situation, aren't I?" She shakes her head but somehow manages to add a smile to her features.

"Not a coward." Mara grabs Lucy's hand and squeezes. "I can't even imagine what coming back here is like for you. You're right. I have no idea what happened or what you are going through, and I'm sorry if it feels like I'm being insensitive."

Lucy worries her lips and seems to want to say something before she stops herself. There are tears in her eyes as she looks toward Mara. "Listen, let's go to this chocolate workshop, okay?

And then...well, then I have another letter for you. I promise to answer any questions you have after that."

Another letter? And she's making her wait?

"How many of these letters are there?"

"Too many, in my opinion," Lucy says.

"Let's skip the class," Mara suggests. She'd rather read the letter and find out everything so she can move forward...so they can both move forward.

"Oh no...taking a chocolate class from a master Chocolatier in Belgium is not something you skip." She glances at the watch on her wrist. "Come on, it's close by, and I don't know about you, but I know I'm going to need that chocolate to get through our talk later." She stands, waiting for Mara to do the same.

"That's playing dirty, you realize that, right? You tease with me answers to my past, but then make me wait...that's simple downright evil." She tries to keep her voice light, like she's only teasing, but...is she really?

Lucy's brows rise at her words. "Evil? Evil is eating all the pralines we're about to make and not leaving you any; that's evil, and I have no problem doing that to you."

"Pralines?" Her favorite chocolate of all time, and Lucy knows it.

"Oh honey, this is the land of pralines, don't you know? That stuff you nibble on back home is nothing compared to what we will eat today. And we're being trained by a master chocolate maker, which is not something everyone can say they get to experience."

Lucy grabs Mara's hand, forcing her to follow along whether she wants to or not, but the moment Lucy says praline, Mara already knows she can forget about the upcoming letter for the next hour or two.

After taking a few more turns, Lucy stops in front of a large brick building with a fenced-in yard and two signs hanging on an iron post. One for a bed and breakfast, one for the chocolate shop.

"Can you imagine staying here? I bet you get chocolates in your room every day," Mara says as they open the gate.

"Bram should add that to his rooms. Bruges is known as a chocolate town, after all. It only makes sense, marketing-wise." Lucy muses as she gazes around. "You know, I had a friend who used to live here. This is the richer section of Bruges, or at least, it used to be. This was once what they'd call a manor, all posh with its furniture. They even had a live-in housekeeper and cook. I wonder where they went?"

They come to the door with a sign for Van Hecke, Master Chocolatier, and Mara pushes it open, surprised to see a room full of people, all looking at them.

"Sorry we're late," she says with obvious embarrassment. She makes her way toward a clear area in the back, where Lucy joins her.

"Where's the rest of the group?" Lucy whispers.

Mara checks the phone and sees Jo-Jo posted a photo of them in a chocolate shop, with the caption *'the best chocolate workshop ever - miss you but we have gifts!'*.

"Um, I think we're in the wrong place," she turns the screen to Lucy. "Should we leave?"

"Welcome, welcome," the man standing by the machines claps his hands together. "Now that we're all here, we can get started." The speaker glances up at the clock on the wall with a pointed look.

Someone walks around, handing out half-filled glasses of champagne to everyone.

"I guess we're staying," Lucy says, clinking her glass to Mara's. "Take a photo and send it to the girls. They'll get a kick out of this."

They take a selfie with the Champagne flutes in hand and send it to the group chat, along with the caption *'the time when Mara and Lucy join the wrong chocolate class...'*

The room they're in isn't overly large, and it's been sectioned off into three distinct areas: one with products on display, one where the chocolate is made and poured into molds, and the back area with more shelves and what looks to be coolers to hold the chocolates.

"My name is Stephen, and I'm the fourth-generation chocolatier in my family. As you can see, we are a small boutique chocolate shop, and very proud of our success. After the lockdown, when there were no tourists, we had to close all our shops and go online, and that was one of the best decisions we'd ever made."

They were asked to wash their hands, and one by one, Mara watched as people dipped their hands in one sink full of soapy water, along with one hand towel to dry their hands.

"Please tell me you brought hand sanitizer with you," Lucy leans over and whispers.

Mara pulls out not only hand sanitizer but also hand wipes. "I'm not sticking my hands in that sink," she says.

"You and me both, sister."

Splitting up into two groups, Mara and Lucy stay with the chocolatier as they are shown how chocolate is tempered using a depositor machine that continually mixes the delicious treat at a constant speed and temperature, then after placing the chocolate in molds, they use a vibrating table to remove any air bubbles, to ensure a smooth even shell.

Everyone gets to create their shells, heating and filling the molds before setting them on the vibrator. Everyone takes their turn without issues until Mara is handed the mold and heater.

"I don't know if I should be trusted with this...knowing me, I'll screw something up," she gives Lucy a nervous smile, thinking about all the other workshops they've done together on various trips.

Mara has a habit of messing things up during cooking classes. Either she breaks dishes by dropping them, mixes salt instead of sugar into items, or breaks eggshells into the mixture...if something is going to happen, it will happen to her.

"You've got this girl," Lucy says, pointing a phone at her.

"You're not taking photos, are you?" Mara asks.

Lucy shakes her head. "No way, this is all on video. Smile for the girls!"

Mara smiles, gives a little wave, then heats the shell with no issues. She fills it, coating her fingers with chocolate, and places it down on the vibrating table, without even thinking about where she set the heating gun. She smells something burning, looks around, and doesn't see anything until Lucy points in horror toward a melting chocolate shell, thanks to the heating gun she'd placed in the wrong place.

"Oh…I'm so sorry," she says as Stephen comes over and tosses the burning mold into the sink.

He shakes his head as if not believing something like this would happen.

"Let's change groups now," he says while Mara stares at the ground, embarrassed.

"Troublemaker, like usual," Lucy teases her softly.

"You'd think we'd learn by now; I shouldn't be doing these classes. Do me a favor, and don't tell the girls, okay?"

Lucy snorts. "Like that's gonna happen. Don't worry, I've got it all on video and was live streaming on Instagram. Like it or not, everyone is going to see it."

Mara groans before heading into the back, where they're shown how to make the pralines.

"Now, in the United States, you might call these truffles, but here, we call them pralines. A little history lesson, if you will…it was a doctor from Belgium who created the first praline, and it was all because he was trying to get his patients to take their medicines. Now tell me, who wouldn't want to take their pill if it was covered in chocolate, right?" He takes a break, glancing at everyone in the small room. "A praline is simply a shelled chocolate with a delicious filling. You can use hazelnut, fruit, cremes…there's no limit to how creative you can be regarding pralines, but the traditional one is made with a hazelnut paste, which is what we will be making today."

One by one, they're shown how they take the hardened shells they'd made earlier and fill them with ganache or gianduja - a blend of hazelnut paste and chocolate. A bottom shell is added and then chilled briefly to set.

Mara sits out on creating her own filled pralines, watching Lucy and the others make theirs instead. Instead, she heads to the shop area and takes one of everything since everything looks amazing. She grabs a few extras of the hazelnut paste and contemplates adding more when Lucy comes behind her and starts laughing.

"What? Tell me you don't want one of everything, too."

"You realize we're in a town with over fifty chocolate shops, right? You could leave some for the others to buy," Lucy nudges her while smiling. "But grab an extra one for me, please."

"Aren't you glad we didn't skip this," Lucy says as they carry their bags down the street.

"I think I'm glad we went to the wrong workshop, but I'm ready for you to give me that next letter," Mara says, reminding the woman of her earlier promise.

"These damn letters. I never should have promised..."

"Promised what?"

"I wanted to tell you everything a long time ago. I've always wanted to be honest with you, to tell you the whole story, but your mother..." Lucy's lips purse together.

"She made you promise not to, I know."

"She thought this would be easier, sharing the story in bits and pieces. I told her it was a stupid idea, but she made me promise...a mother knows best, or some crap like that."

"She's not here now, you realize that, right?"

"You think I'm going to betray a promise I made on a woman's deathbed? She'll haunt me for the rest of my life."

"Oh, come on, Lucy. This is ridiculous."

"I agree." She reaches into her purse and pulls out an envelope.

"Let's stop for lunch. Shari told me of a place with the best waffles I know you'll love."

They head down a street and stop in front of Lizzie's Waffles, waiting their turn for a seat. They are offered one inside, and while Lucy orders for them, Mara focuses on the letter in her hands.

Chapter Twenty-Five

Mara

I'm trying to imagine what you are doing right now, what you know or don't know, and what's happened.

I'm not playing fair, and I know that.

I'm imagining you in Bruges and you've bought more than enough chocolate to last you through the cold winter months. Don't forget to grab some ornaments for the tree, and don't be too upset with me, okay?

I asked Lucy to make me a promise, but I have never expected her to keep that promise after my death, so I'm going to assume you know everything by now.

I'm sorry. This wasn't how I wanted you to learn things.

Truth be told, I never wanted you to know any of this in the first place.

That family...isn't your family. They aren't your roots. The only family you need is the one already in place - Lucy, Lily, and Gus, everyone in our community at home.

Lucas and Bram...they aren't your family. They never wanted to be part of your family, never wanted you in their lives. Regardless of what they say, regardless of the stories they've told you, it was made very clear to me that we were not welcomed in their lives.

I have the proof, Mara. Lucas paid for me to leave, go home, and never contact his son again. He gave me a letter, confirming that the man you think as your father, wanted nothing to do with you.

I made the only choice possible for us both. It was the only way to survive the heartache, to move on without the past holding us down and hurting us.

Some memories aren't worth living with.

Some memories are best broken and destroyed.

Trust me, Mara. I know it's not what you want to hear, I know it's not the answers you were hoping for. I hate that you are even needing answers.

I tried telling Lucy that opening this door would only bring you heartbreak, and that's the last thing I've ever wanted for you.

I hope you'll forgive me. Forgive me for asking you to take this trip. Forgive me for forcing these doors to open. Forgive me for listening to Lucy when she said you deserved to know the truth. I'm sorry if I made a mistake in thinking this trip would give you any answers and close any doors Lucy forced open.

I love you, Mara-mine.

I hope you'll never forget that.

Mom

PS...I did write your father letters, telling him about you, and sharing photographs of you, but he never once responded to me. Eventually, I stopped writing, stopped caring about his silence. He made it clear he didn't want to be part of your life. That told me all I needed to know and confirmed that we didn't need him. We had each other, and that's all we needed.

Chapter Twenty-Six

"Mom thinks you've already told me everything." Mara sets the letter down on the table, pushing it toward Lucy for her to read.

Lucy shakes her head as she reads the letter.

"That woman," she mutters as the server approaches with their coffee and waffles.

Mara glances down at her dish and groans with delight. It's a thick and crispy square waffle covered in fresh cut strawberries and Nutella, with a bowl of whipped cream on the side.

"Looks delicious, doesn't it," Lucy says as she hands back the letter. "Let this old woman eat in peace, and then I'll tell you everything I know, okay?"

Everything always seems to be on Lucy's timing, she's always having to wait until Lucy is ready to talk.

"You're not so old that you can't talk and eat simultaneously."

Lucy cuts into her waffle, taking a bite, a look on her face daring Mara to object.

She sighs instead and then takes a bite of her own waffle.

"Wow." One bite of the crispy, light, and airy waffle, and she wants more.

"The secret is to use carbonated water," their server said with a wink as she walked by.

"That's it. That's all I'm using from now on," Mara says as she spoons more whipped cream onto a piece and takes another bite.

"I can't believe your mother wouldn't trust me to keep my word," Lucy finally says. "Do you have any idea how hard it's been?"

"So why did you?"

Lucy sets her fork down on her plate. "Because telling you the truth also meant facing my own demons, and maybe a part of me wasn't ready for that."

How is she supposed to respond to that? Call Lucy out on her selfishness? What would that do? The woman already knows she's in the wrong, right?

"I'm not going to excuse myself, Mara. Neither one of us deserves that lack of respect. I could have done many things - refused to come on this trip, refused to give you the letters, refused to tell you the truth...but again, that wouldn't have been right for either of us."

Lucy looks off to the side, lost in her memories. Mara gives her time to work through whatever battle she's inwardly fighting. "Coming back here is hard, and I've been preparing myself for that since Kat told me my flight was already paid for. Deep down, I think I've always known that telling you the truth is worth it."

"Why?"

"Why what?" Lucy looks confused.

"Why is it worth it?"

"Good question. Why is it worth dealing with my own ghosts? Worth seeing the hurt in your eyes? Worth having to bear the weight that should be placed on your mother's shoulders?" She lifts her shoulder in a shrug. "Because I think you deserve to know the truth. I think we both deserve the truth. I don't know if it's possible now, after all this time, but...I'm hoping we'll figure it out."

"Lucy, talk plain, please, rather than in circles."

"We're relying on the broken memories of the past, Mara. From both your mother and my father."

"What about my father? Where does he fit in all this?"

Lucy heaves a sigh as she pushes her half-eaten waffle to the side.

"Jules died when you were maybe...three years old, I think?" Lucy shakes her head, her bearing heavy with a heaviness Mara understands all too well. "At the time, his death seemed pointless. He was out driving on a back road, going too fast around a corner, and he flipped his car. He died instantly, from what we were told."

A little dart of sadness fills Mara. "That must have been hard for you."

"Our family broke apart when he died." The still-present grief in Lucy's voice brought tears to Mara's eyes. "Death is never easy to process and something you never get over. Not even if you have time to prepare yourself. Jules was the baby of the family, and even though he was my brother, Bram and I raised him after our mother's death. I swore I never wanted to feel that level of grief again, which is probably why I've never had children of my own."

"I'm so sorry." Mara reaches out for Lucy's hand.

"Oh, sweetheart, don't waste your tears. Remember, I said at the time it seemed pointless. Wait until you hear the full story."

"When did he find out about me? Mom said she had a letter from him..."

All it takes is one look on Lucy's face for Mara to fall silent.

"Your mother...she left out of the blue. I think I told you this, right? We planned on joining a ghost walk one night, and when I went to her room to tell her it was time to leave, she was already gone. Bags packed, no note, no nothing. Jules didn't even know. When he came home and found her gone, he was in a funk for weeks. He was a bear, mopping around like a lost puppy dog. He loved your mother, Mara, in a young love, first love sort of way. It was cute, and we teased him about it...until she left and broke his heart."

"I...I don't get it. Mom's letters—"

"Your mother was hurting; you need to remember that. From the time your mother left to the time I saw you both in Paris...well, I guess the term nowadays is, she ghosted us. To be honest, we all eventually forgot about Stella, too. I mean, every so often, Jules would bring her up, and we'd listen to his puppy dog story and soothe his broken heart yet again, but that was it."

"Did he ever marry?"

Lucy shakes her head. "He fell hard and fast for Stella and never quite got over her. Maybe he would have, eventually...but he died too young."

Mara lets it all settle, working everything out so she can understand things properly.

"So, Mom basically came, fell in love, and you and her were besties until she up and disappeared. Julian never got over her, and he died three years later. You moved on with your life until you saw me in Paris, and then...what? What happened?"

"What do you remember?"

"After Paris? We said goodbye, you and Mom kept in contact, and the next thing I know, you're in our apartment for a visit."

"A visit that never ended. It's a good thing I married an American. Living in Seattle, it's a quick flight to Calgary, which meant I could visit anytime, but also that I wasn't that close where your mother felt smothered."

"But what happened exactly? Bram said something about you cutting a visit short, storming out, and saying this family was dead to you. What happened?"

"What happened was Paris. What happened was I found out about you, and my life changed in that moment. I came home, so excited to tell my father, only to find out he always knew about you. He knew, and he didn't care."

Mara sits back in her chair, unsure how to take this.

"It wasn't just that," Lucy says, all color draining from her face. "The day my brother died, he found out about you, found out that our father had kept you a secret, and he left here determined to find you. He was on his way to the airport when he died."

"But his letter?" If he just found out, when would he have had time to write it and ... oh no...so many things start to click for Mara and there's a flame of anger that bursts bright, wanting to scorch all the sadness inside her.

Lucy closes her eyes. "I blame my father for so many things - for placing too much responsibility on my young shoulders after my mother's death, for being cold and distant...but most of all, I blame him for destroying our family," her eyes open and she stares directly at Mara, "by keeping you a secret," she finishes.

Chapter Twenty-Seven

"I'm ready to go home."

Mara says the heavy words as they take their time walking through the streets of Brugge. The place truly is beautiful with its historical fairytale atmosphere, but it's lost on Mara, and rather than spend another day here, she'd rather leave.

Leave all of this - the secrets, the family that never wanted her, all of it. She now understands why Stella always said family is who you choose to be in your life. She has all the family she needs back home.

As they walk along Steenstraat, Mara barely notices all the chocolate shops they pass by. In fact, if it weren't for Lucy stopping and pulling her hand, she would have walked right past Sandra and Jo-Jo, who stood outside of the Pierre Marcolini shop.

"Oh hey, you two," Jo-Jo says as she wraps her arm through Mara's. "Remember when you sent me that video of the little gnomes opening up an advent calendar, and I said we had to find that shop and buy one? Well, guess what?" She points to the window display where there's a display of advent calendars and little gnomes with tall pointy hats playing amongst the boxes and chocolates. "Come on, we have to get one."

Mara finds herself being pulled into the store.

"They really are cute, aren't they?" She doesn't hesitate to pick up one of the calendars. She adds some macarons and even more pralines to her growing pile of goods.

"Is everything okay?" Jo-Jo asks. "I haven't wanted to say anything, I know you've got Lucy and Sandra to talk to, but...I'm here, okay?"

Mara rests her head on Jo-Jo's shoulder for a second before she gives her friend a wobbly smile. "Thank you." It means more than she thought it would to have Jo-Jo say that.

They might be the closest in age within the group, but Mara has always felt they were the furthest apart when it comes to their friendship. They are so different - Jo-Jo is on her fourth marriage, a socialite from New York, while Mara is still single, living in a small Canadian town overtop a bookstore.

When they leave the shop, they find Sandra and Lucy deep in discussion, and rather than intrude, they meander down the street, window shopping, taking in the quaint and utterly European displays.

"The town is cute, isn't it? I'd love to explore it when it's not so busy, though," Jo-Jo says as she eyes a dress in a window. "They've definitely embraced the tourists, that's for sure. At the chocolate workshop, someone mentioned that the town is quiet at night once everyone leaves. I guess Bruges is mainly a day trip experience for most people. Oh, and hey, where did you guys end up? How did you not find us?" Jo-Jo finally takes a breath.

"Don't ask me. Lucy was the one with the map."

"And they didn't check your name? Didn't want to see your voucher for the class?"

Mara shakes her head. "We were a bit late, and the instructor seemed a little...impatient. He probably regrets it, though, especially after I almost set the place on fire."

At Jo-Jo's gasp, Lucy and Sandra join them, and Lucy rolls her eyes when she hears Mara's slight over-exaggeration.

"It was one chocolate mold that got slightly melted, that's it. It's their fault for offering glasses of champagne beforehand." The smile on her lips doesn't quite make up to her eyes.

"Okay, what is going on?" Jo-Jo re-adjusts her purse before crossing her arms. "The two of you have been in a mood this whole trip, and I know it's more than just you missing your mother and you," she points at Lucy, "returning home."

"Jo-Jo…" Sandra offers a warning in her voice, but Jo-Jo wants nothing to do with it, from how she waves a hand.

"If it's none of my business, say so, but I have a feeling you already know, and it's not fair to the rest of us to keep us in the dark. The trip isn't the same without the two of you, I hope you know that."

Mara glances over to Lucy. Jo-Jo's right.

"Where is everyone else?" Lucy asks instead.

With a huff, Jo-Jo pulls out her phone. "They are over in Simon Stevin Square, where there's another market. It looks like it's at the end of this street."

Lucy glances at her phone and then nods. "How about we go join everyone? Tonight at dinner, Mara and I have something to share. Do you mind waiting that long? To be honest, having to repeat this and answer the same questions will be more than I can handle."

Jo-Jo crosses her arms, obviously upset at being kept in the dark. "I don't have a choice, do I?" She heads off at a march that leaves everyone else rushing to catch up.

Not much is said as they make their way down the street together. Jo-Jo isn't as frosty toward them by the time they meet up with the others, but she's also not as cheerful as she usually is either.

The market here is a little smaller than the one in the main market square, but huts are decorated the same, with the Linden trees wrapped in twinkling fairy lights.

"There's a different feel to the markets in the day, don't you think?" Donna and Kat are standing by a hut serving gluwein and Jenever. "Plus, I think we're all a little out of sorts. I think we all need to do a few shots. Apparently, doing shots of Jenever at the markets is quite the Belgium thing." She points to the rows of shot glasses lined up along the edge of the display.

Mara steps up and orders a round for everyone. "This is on Stella," she says as she raises her glass in a toast. "If ever there was a trip my mother should have been on, it's this one."

"Ain't that the truth," Lucy mutters as she downs her shot. "Now, to be clear, it's not just the Belgian thing to do a few shots at the markets. You are supposed to go from stall to stall and order a shot from each vendor until you can barely stand straight. You'll notice the glasses are small, right? That's because the alcohol percentage is like 38 percent or something. It takes a strong Flemish constitution to do this tradition right."

"It's a little too early in the day to do that, I think," Kat says as she places her glass on a tray. "Plus, I'm not a gin fan, so I'm out."

They continue to do a little more market shopping, with Mara buying some uber soft lamb wool skeins for Lily and then finding a distinct Bruges ornament for Gus to hang on one of the bookshop trees. He likes to keep one tree for all the ornaments she and Stella would bring home for him as gifts.

"I'm ready to head back to the B&B for a little relaxing, what do you guys say? We've almost hit ten thousand steps today, and my feet need a break." Kat suggests as they all meet at the end of the market.

The last thing Mara wants to do is return to the B&B, but then she remembers that there's a wedding reception happening, and the likelihood of seeing Bram or anyone else, for that matter, is slim.

She can see Lucy thinking the same thing. "A little siesta with a good book sounds perfect," Mara says.

She still wants to go home, and maybe after dinner, once everyone understands what is going on, the others will understand.

Chapter Twenty-Eight

Back at Barabas, Mara stands at the window and looks down over the backyard. The bride and groom are taking photos beneath a lighted archway while the rest of the crowd mingle. All the women appear to be wearing heavy shawls or fur-lined coats over their dresses.

"Listen," Mara turns around and looks at Lucy, who's reclining on her bed. "I'm serious about leaving early. We don't have to stay here, right? I mean, I get the other might not want to leave so soon, but we don't have to go home or anything. Paris is a quick train ride away, or we could go to Germany or...or anywhere really. Maybe we can do that chocolate train in Switzerland instead? Anywhere but here."

Lucy drops the book she's holding in her hand and frowns. "We're not running anywhere, although a trip through the Swiss Alps on the hunt for chocolate is something your mother would approve of, but I think that's a completely different trip and only runs during specific months of the year. Besides, we are not leaving until you meet Lucas."

"We've already been over that," Mara says, reiterating a comment she'd said as they finished up their waffles earlier. "I don't want to meet him." Especially not after realizing he probably wrote that fake letter to her mother. "Stella was right. He's not my grandfather. He's not my family. You are."

"Then say that to him. Say it, and then we'll leave, even if the others decide to stay here." Lucy rolls her neck ever so slowly, her joints cracking extra loud. "Trust me, if you don't meet him, if you don't get off your chest the things you need to say, you'll always regret it."

"What's to regret? Meeting a man who never cared about me in the first place? I don't need to give someone like that space in my life."

"Then do it for me," Lucy says slowly, with a heaviness Mara can feel. "Your mother was right, as much as I hate to admit it. This trip is as much for me as it is for you."

"Then take your own advice, Lucy. Stop running and see your father. Say whatever it is you need to say and do whatever you need to do for your own healing. I'm out. Done. Whatever you and Mom thought this trip would do for me, it's over."

"Mara." Lucy's voice is tinged with disappointment and sadness.

Mara knows that voice; she knows what it means, and she doesn't care.

"I need a strong cappuccino. I think I saw a cafe around the corner. Do you want one?"

"Why don't you grab one from downstairs?" Lucy asks.

"And possibly run into your brother or even your father? No, thank you." She grabs her purse and wraps a scarf around her neck.

Mara heads down the stairs and is about to open the door when she notices someone standing to the side. She places her hand on the knob and slowly turns, not wanting to bring attention to her exit. Her brain is swirling with so many thoughts and emotions; having Bram notice her is the last thing she wants.

"Mara, you're back."

When she glances over at him, he gives her a smile full of hope and desperation, she can't help but drop her hand from the doorknob.

"Hi, sorry, I don't mean to bother you. I was about to head out for a coffee."

"Why go out? You know you can make one here. Come, let me make it for you instead."

"I don't want to be a bother," she says as she gestures to the crowds outside. "I know you have an event happening and..."

"And nothing. We have people taking care of them, and I've already closed off the doors to the kitchen, so it's not a bother at all." He stands still, as if waiting to see what she'll do. He probably expects her to run.

Running is what she wants to do.

"Okay, well...thank you," she says. She recently accused Lucy of running from this family. Why make the same mistake?

"I was hoping to see you, actually. I found something last night that I wanted to share with you."

Intrigued, she follows him into the kitchen, where she sees a box on the table.

"Please, look inside," Bram says.

Curious, she removes the lid and finds a stack of notebooks inside.

"I found some of Julian's journals from when he met your mother. I thought you might enjoy going through them."

Everything inside her wants to pour through those books right that instant, but she manages to pull back on that impulse and instead, lifts the books, one by one, out and stacks them on the table.

She holds one in her hand but hesitates. She's holding her father's journals in her hands. She'd just told Lucy she was done with all of this...and yet...

Inside these journals are her father's personal thoughts and feelings. She knows her mother's side of the story - somewhat. She knows Lucy's. Maybe through her father's eyes, she'll get a better sense of the truth?

What is it her mother always said about learning the truth? *It's supposed to hurt. That's what makes it real.*

Is she ready? She's already learned enough, enough for the pain to be constant and lingering. Does she want to add more to it? Should she add more to it?

The answer is there as she opens the journal and notices the dates. One journal per year.

This one is a year after her birth. She opens another, then another, until she finds the one from when her mother would have been here.

The first thing she notices is his handwriting. It's smooth, legible, and very neat. Neater than her own, that's for sure.

She rustles through the pages until she finds roughly when her mother should have been at the bed and breakfast.

A smile kisses her lips as she reads her father's description from when he first met Stella. He was enthralled, entranced, and experienced instant love with just one look.

Mara has never believed in love at first sight, but reading his words, she believes he fell in love hard for her mother.

"Oh good, you're reading the first one," Bram says as he joins her at the table, placing a cup topped with whipped cream in front of her. "I made you a mocha, hope that was okay?" He points to the journal in her hand. "Jules was a young pup who fell so hard for Stella. Your mother fell just as hard for him. You could see it. They couldn't keep their eyes or hands off each other, and she was all he would talk about. We'd be in our bedroom, me trying to fall asleep, and he'd yammer on and on about her until I would beg him to shut up." Bram chuckles at the memory. "I'd give anything to hear his voice again..."

Bram sits with her and reaches for his own coffee. "Are you okay with some company, or would you prefer to be alone?"

Mara doesn't look up from the journal in her hand. "Did you read these?"

"I read that one, yes." He takes a sip of his coffee before he pushes his chair away. "I sent Lucy a message and asked her to join us. This avoidance is ridiculous."

Laughter from the group outside fills the air. "Do you hold a lot of parties like this one?"

"I try. The extra income helps. We do okay as a bed and breakfast; we have a lot of repeat customers as well, but thanks to the lockdown, we had to use up a bit of our savings." He shrugs. "At least we didn't have to close up like many others did. That reminds me, how did your chocolate workshop go?"

It takes her a moment to register his words. She drags her gaze from the pages and forces herself to focus.

"The workshop was great. We both came home with way too much chocolate, which isn't that much of a problem, right?"

He laughs. "I hope you brought an extra duffel bag with you?"

"One of my mom's top ten tips for traveling to Europe," she says. "Mom wrote a little book full of travel tips and tricks. A foldable luggage bag for all those extra little things you buy that otherwise won't fit in your luggage is essential."

"That doesn't surprise me. From what I remember about Stella, she was a woman of many talents."

"You have no idea who Stella was," Lucy says, startling them as she joins them at the table. "That woman could have run circles around the three of us without breaking a sweat." She pulls out a chair and sits. "The girl you remember and the woman she became are two completely different people."

She leans across the table and grabs one of the notebooks. "These look familiar." She opens. "It's Jules journals. Why are you...?" Her voice trails off as she flips through the book. "Oh, wow." She leans back in her chair, pulling the journal tight to her chest.

"Yeah, it hit me hard last night," Bram says. "Brought back a lot of memories."

"More like neatly boxed skeletons Dad stores in his closet. That's where you found these, right?" Lucy's right brow rises so high it's hidden beneath her bangs.

"Lucy, come on. Don't go there, okay?" Bram turns his back as he starts up the cappuccino machine.

"So, what, we run now when anyone brings up the past?" Lucy asks.

"I don't run when I get bad news. I'll leave that to you." The bitterness in Bram's voice could peel paint off walls.

Mara tries to become a wallflower, observing but unobserved at the same time.

"Ouch," Lucy mumbles. "How long have you been holding that one in?" She shakes her head as she lowers the journal to the table. "I left for a reason. I didn't run. I just left and have never returned, not till now."

"What's with the whole skeletons in the closet comment?" Mara keeps her voice down.

"Yes," someone else says. "What was that about?" His words, in stilted English, sound twisted and warped.

Mara looks over to find an older man standing in the doorway. He's wearing a blue wool cardigan, half buttoned up, with plain grey pants and black slippers. His hands are playing with the ends of a scarf wrapped around his neck.

Lucy sighs. "Hello, Father."

Chapter Twenty-Nine

This is the man that changed so much of her mother's life? She forces herself to hold on to the anger that has been burning inside her ever since she realized the role he's played in her missing out on having a father in her life, but it's hard when she sees how fragile he is.

Lucy doesn't move for the longest time. It's like she's frozen in place, the shock of seeing Lucas is almost too much for her.

Mara reaches over and squeezes Lucy's hand and that's all it takes. Lucy gives out a loud sob as she pushes her chair out and rushes over to give her ailing father a hug.

She watches as the strong, supportive, stubborn woman in front of her crumbles in her father's arms. She watches as a father comforts his long-lost daughter, his eyes closing with a sense of fullness and forgiveness.

Mara's heart aches for that hug. Not from Lucas, but from her mother. She aches for her mother's hug, for the strength behind that comfort, comfort she'll never feel again.

Life has not been playing nice with her at all.

Earlier, she told Lucy she didn't want to meet Lucas - that she didn't need to meet him. Her walls are up, and she is not only aware of that, but she's okay with it. Why meet someone who never wanted to meet her? Why open herself up to that?

Yet, seeing Lucy and Lucas together, the way the man's arms wrap around his daughter and don't seem to want to let go... maybe he's not so coldhearted after all? Maybe he has his own regrets, regrets that have been years in the making.

She tries to ignore the murmurings between father and daughter. She can't understand the words, but the emotion is visceral enough that her eyes swim in tears.

It takes a few moments before she realizes her name is being called. When she looks up, Lucy stands at her father's side, her arm linked with his, with questions on both faces.

She also notices the way Lucas seems to lean on Lucy like he needs support.

Mara pushes herself to her feet and awkwardly holds a hand toward a man who should mean nothing to her.

"Mara, this is Lucas, my father. He'd like to sit and chat for a moment if that would be okay?" There's a pleading in Lucy's gaze, and Mara can't help but nod.

Lucas takes her hand, his gesture frail, his handshake not as firm as she expects.

"Welcome to our home," Lucas says, his voice catching as he drops her hand.

Lucy pulls out a seat for him before sitting down herself.

No one says anything, the silence stretching into uncomfortable.

Lucas reaches out, his hands shaky, as he touches a notebook from the middle of the table. His jaw is unsteady, his lips quivering, as his fingers brush across the cover.

"Life has a way of coming full circle," Lucas says, his gaze never leaving the notebook. "Every decision made, every choice contemplated, every action taken will always come back to you, in one form or another, demanding justification." He wipes the tears still on his face, then looks to Lucy.

"My actions cost me my family." He reaches out and pats his daughter's hands, the joy at seeing her so clear in his gaze. He then turns to Mara. "My decisions destroyed so many futures."

He looks around the room, at Mara and Lucy sitting beside him, at Bram, who stands at the counter, his head bowed as if hiding his own tears.

"We have tried to make the best out of the life we've been given. My choices have affected everyone here, but I can't apologize for any of that. What happened, happened. There's no changing it. There's no going backward. We've lost so much because of what I did, and I've carried the weight without complaining. My choices. My actions. My consequences."

Lucy snorts. She leans back in her chair and shakes her head. "Yes, you can apologize, Father. And you should. Apologize for the secrets you kept from all of us. For the future you stole from us. You should apologize for that." Her words are harsh, but she softens the blow by keeping her voice low and mild.

"Every single one of us has made mistakes." Bram places a coffee in front of Lucy, a cup of water in front of Lucas, and hands Mara a plate with a puff pastry full of whipped cream and chocolate. "I can't speak for Mara; I feel very protective of her and don't want to see her hurt more than necessary. But that being said—"

"But nothing," Lucy interjects. "Mara is innocent in all of this."

"And shouldn't be subject to the family skeletons," Lucas adds.

"Whoa, hold on here." Mara leans forward and plants a palm on the table. "I'm not a child to ignore," she says to Lucas, "or someone who needs protecting," she looks to Bram as she says this. "Whether you like it or not, I am a member of this family, but that doesn't mean I want to be part of all this." She draws a circle in the air, starting at Bram and ending with herself.

"Of course, you are part of us," Bram says, his brows furrowed in confusion. "What do you mean by that?"

Mara tries to think of a response, but Lucy reaches out with a hand, stopping her.

"Why would she want to be?" Lucy says. "Seriously, Bram, think about it. Family is who you choose to be in your life, not who has to be."

"And what does that mean? Family is family. Family is blood. Family isn't chosen."

"Oh, Bram, as naive as always. How can you not understand?"

"But you're here. You choose to come here and meet us," Bram directs this to Mara. "I would assume that means you want to know more about us, about your family. Am I wrong?"

"Of course you are," Lucy answers, her voice rising with anger and frustration. "She didn't even know about you, about what all this means until we got here."

Mara holds up a hand, the chaotic vibes swirling around this table too much for her. "Stop, please, both of you."

Lucas pushes his chair back and stands. "Mara, there is something I'd like to show you. I think my children have some issues to take care of, and we don't need to be here in the midst of it. Would you join me, please?" He holds out a hand, waiting to see if she'll accept.

Without thought, she stands but doesn't take his hand. She snatches a piece of chocolate off her plate, plopping it in her mouth before she lets Lucas guide her through the house and into an area she hasn't yet seen.

"This is our personal quarters," Lucas explains. "I hope you don't mind me taking you from the other two. There is a lot for them to discuss and decide on, but...I feel you deserve to have all the information before you make any choices."

"What kind of information?"

He leads her through the house until they come to a closed door.

"It's probably best if your mother explains it herself."

Chapter Thirty

Caught off guard, Mara stumbles and grabs onto the doorframe for support.

"Excuse me?" She glances around in wonder and amazement. Of all the rooms she expected to walk into - this is not it. It's a Christmas library, an actual Christmas library, and the moment Mara steps into the room, she feels like she's been transported back to her childhood.

How is this possible?

For someone who lives and breathes life within a bookstore, there's an element of comfort and familiarity within this room for her. She's being wrapped in coziness and peace, in childhood delights and a revolving turntable of memories from her life as a child that it's like being sucker punched by Santa Clause himself.

There are no words as she walks through the room, stopping at everything, needing to touch it all.

Unwrap the Christmas from this room, and it would be a standard sitting room complete with a fireplace, and wall-covered bookshelves overflowing with books and knickknacks. There's a small desk in one corner, a couch, two chairs, and a coffee table in the middle of the room. Add in the holiday decor, and there's a lighted Christmas tree in the corner with a wooden train set winding its way along the tree skirt, stockings over the fireplace, and garland on every surface. There's even a nativity scene sitting on the fireplace mantle.

On the walls are framed drawings of everything winter and Christmas, drawings that steal Mara's breath because she recognizes them as her own.

The bookshelves are full of not just books but of childhood Christmas stories her mother used to read to her, handmade ornaments and decorations a child would make in school, and tiny black sheep set in every nook and cranny.

Black sheep. The one thing she loves to collect. The one thing she's never known anyone else to collect like her.

"Lucas...what is all this?"

"Huh? My own little slice of Christmas. Do you like it? I call it my Christmas Library." He doesn't look at her, in fact, his back is to her as he shuffles through various books, pulling them out, and riffling through the pages.

"I thought I put them all here," he mutters.

Christmas Library. This is a library full of her memories. Why does he have this stuff? Why is it here?

"Lucas, how did you get this?" She takes a frame off the wall and holds it out to him, wanting, needing him to turn around and answer her.

It's a drawing she made when she might have been six or seven. It's of her and her mom, standing beside an outdoor Christmas tree. There's snow on the ground and there's even a black sheep standing beside her. She's holding hands with her mom and they both have bright red smiles on their faces.

She remembers drawing this. She has this vague memory of sitting at the kitchen table with a handful of drawings and Stella telling her to pick her favorite one to send to Santa.

She always drew pictures for Santa.

Except, they obviously didn't go to Santa, did they? They came here.

"Lucas, how did you get this?" There's an insistence in her voice that has Lucas turning.

"Oh, yes, from your mother. She sent them every year for the longest time. I found them all a few years ago. It might be too late to go back in time and redo mistakes, but...I can at least honor these memories, no?"

Honor these memories?

"Did my mother send them to you?" Mara finds that highly unlikely, if that's the case.

"Oh no, she wouldn't do that. She hated me, and rightly so. She sent these to Julian, she sent a lot of things over the years to him, until one day she stopped. He never saw them though, well... not all of them." He turns and continues his search.

"They should all be right here. I know I put them here," he reaches where she's standing and nudges her to the side as he pulls out more books and riffles through them.

"Um...Lucas, what are you looking for?" She watches in bewilderment as the older man grows more agitated. "Maybe I should get Bram?" She glances toward the door, praying the man himself will appear.

"How well did you know your mother?" Lucas asks, pivoting the conversation.

"Better than you," Mara says, caught off guard and slightly aggravated by the question.

All of this: the room, her drawings, the sheep...it's all too overwhelming and full of too many unanswered questions.

"Why the black sheep?" She asks, turning the conversation back.

"Because you like them. Every time I find one, I think of you." He shakes his head at her as if the answer is obvious.

"I think you'll find, when it comes to our parents, we don't know them at all." He purses his lips and whistles.

She sighs with obvious frustration. "What are you talking about?"

"My children, even as adults, view me through the lenses of their childish memories. They judge me by those same memories," he says with sadness. "They treat me as they remember how I treated them. No matter how old we are, we never outgrow our childish views when it comes to our parents."

"I don't agree."

He shrugs. "It doesn't matter if you agree or not. Throughout the test of time, this is always how it is."

He moves his attention to another level of the bookshelf, pulling out a book at a time until he makes a grunt. "Found them… Well, I found one." He holds up a weathered envelope and waves it in the air.

"You read this while I find the others. I know they're in here someplace."

Mara takes the letter he holds out and recognizes her mother's handwriting.

"What is this?" It feels like this is all she's been asking since meeting him.

"Isn't it obvious? A letter your mother wrote."

"But why is it here, hidden in a book?"

"I'm not as cold-hearted as my daughter seems to believe I am. When that first letter arrived, I wasn't sure if giving it to Julian was smart. She broke my son's heart."

"She broke his heart?"

"He was too young to fall in love. Too young to be a father. Too young for all that kind of responsibility. I don't know what your mother has told you about him, but it's only half the truth."

She blinks, not believing what she's hearing. "My mother has told me nothing about him. In fact, I didn't even know he existed until recently."

He shakes his head with clicking his tongue. "Now, that doesn't surprise me. Your mother was a stubborn one."

A thin ribbon of anger pulls within Mara's body until she's tighter than an arrow about to be launched. She's not sure how to take this man. She's not even sure she likes him. She takes a seat on the couch, her shoulders pushed back and lifts the envelope flap, pulling out the letter from inside.

She tells herself this is no different than the letters Lucy gives her, but the truth is, this is very different.

This isn't a letter meant for her. It's not a letter that will explain what she needs to know. It's a letter that will show her more of her mother and reveal intimate details about her parents that she's not sure she wants to know.

"But why hide it in a book?" She asks the question, needing extra time, maybe even extra strength, to read it.

"Ahh, well, when it arrived, I wasn't sure what to do. Giving it to Julian wasn't an option, not at first. You don't understand how fragile he was...as his father, I had to look out for him, protect him. However, I'm not so coldhearted as to throw it away or burn it in the fireplace. While I was considering what to do, he came in here, wanting to talk about...something. I can't remember now. In my rush, I hid it. The thing about Julian...he loved books. He loved to read, to write...he fancied himself a writer and wanted to be an English teacher, maybe even one day write his own great novel." Lucas shakes his head. "My son's head was full of dreams, he never lived in the real world."

Mara frowns, not liking his words or his attitude about his son. His deceased son. Her father.

"I figured he'd eventually find it if it were meant to be. I firmly believe that life has a way of opening doors when the time is right. Look at you, here, now. And with my daughter. It's a wish come true. But, with Julian, if he was meant to know about you, he'd find the letter. Or, letters." He pulls out another book and retrieves a second letter from inside.

"How many are there?"

Lucas lifts his shoulder, indicating the answer isn't important.

"Feel free to look through and see if there are more. If you're to find them, you will."

She jolts when he places a hand on her shoulder, giving a slight squeeze before he leaves the room.

"Enjoy my library of memories."

Chapter Thirty-One

Curling up on the couch, giving the door one last glance, Mara smooths out the letter against her leg, her finger going over the crease one, two, three times.

My dearest Julian,

It's hard to continue, even just reading those three words.

Mara thinks back to the letters her mother wrote her, how she said she never contacted her father. She obviously lied. She did write him. She wrote him multiple times, even sending him things she made over the years.

Why the lie? Why not admit the truth?

Before all of this, before the dementia took over their lives, Mara would have said her mother never lied to her. Stella made it clear that honesty and truth were paramount in all things. Truth is easier to remember than lies. Lies tangle you up and have a way of catching you off guard. With the truth, you never have to worry about what story you told and to whom.

So, none of this makes sense.

The letter in her hands reveals more of the love story between her parents. It also reveals the heartache Stella lived within that first year.

Julian, I left with a secret, a secret your father made me promise not to tell you, but that's not right. You need to know. You deserve to know. Julian, we're having a baby!

Coming back to Belgium isn't something I can do. I will never return to Belgium, that's a promise, but maybe you'll come to Canada? Our baby deserves to be loved by both parents, and I know, after the shock wears off, that being a father is something you will be amazing at.

You said you wanted children one day. I know this is a little fast-paced and sooner than you'd anticipated, but you'll be an amazing father to our child, Julian. All your fears of being the father you have won't come true, I know it. You're nothing like your father. Nothing.

I don't know if we're having a boy or a girl. I hope it's a girl. I know you wanted girls, too. She'll be our little Christmas baby, our very own Christmas gift.

He wanted to have a little girl? So they talked about having kids? That means they discussed the future, a future together, one that included her.

The rest of the letter is her mother apologizing for leaving like she did and asking him to write back.

She signs off by saying she loved Julian with everything inside her, and being away from him was like losing a part of her soul. She begged him to come to Canada so she could feel complete again.

None of this sounded like the woman she grew up with.

"There you are," Lucy interrupts her musings. "W...wow, look at this room. I...I never knew my father loved Christmas this much." She walks in and heads toward the wall where many of Mara's drawings are framed. It's a whole wall of her framed drawings. Just one more thing she's struggling to process.

"Are these...?" Lucy continues while Mara sits in silence. "I don't remember doing these. Why would he put them...to Santa, love Mara. Um..." The look of shock and disbelief on her face must match the one on Mara's.

"I can't wrap my head around it either." Mara places the letter she was reading down in her lap.

"Why does my father have your drawings for Santa?"

Mara shrugs. "My mother sent them. I think to Julian, but he never got them."

"Your mother sent my brother your drawings. Huh."

"And your father hid those drawings and letters in his books." Mara lets out a long and torturous sigh, feeling extremely exhausted and overwhelmed. This whole trip has been overwhelming and not in a good way.

Lucy collapses beside her. "So, he still does that. He started that after my mother's death. No...he did it before, to be honest. He used to leave her little notes in books for her to find. But after she passed away, he started squirreling other things away, like bills and stuff. I think it was his way of not dealing with things, which looking back, is probably the truth. Bram says he's worse at it now."

Lucy reaches for one of the letters in his lap. "What's this?"

"It's a letter from my mother." There's a heaviness in her words that settles deep within her heart.

"From Stella? To Lucas?"

Mara shakes her head. "To my father," she whispers.

"Oh, honey...Stella, why did you have to make this so difficult?" She mutters softly. "Can I read it?" Lucy takes her time reading the words from one lover to another, her lips forming the silent words, her head shaking at times as the things her mother reveals.

"Did you find this?" Lucy finally asks.

"Lucas gave it to me. He said I deserved to know the truth from my mother herself."

Lucy sighs. "So, when she said she never contacted him, she was lying."

Mara nods. "She obviously was lying about a lot of things. Why this, though?" She takes back the letter and waves it.

"I don't know honey, I really don't. Maybe lie is the wrong word. She might have just forgotten. Maybe…maybe this was a memory she didn't want to remember."

"But she was lucid when she wrote me the letters, right? In her first one, she said she was having good days, and I gathered you were there with her when she was writing them. You would have known, right? If she was fully herself or not?"

"I was…and I don't recall anything noticeable. She'd ask me certain things, but I thought it was to clarify in her own mind that she was remembering the right things. You know what it was like… especially in the beginning when she would confuse things."

"Her stories would be half-truth and half-something she'd heard or read somewhere."

"You're saying she didn't remember writing him?" Mara would like to hold on to that truth, but she feels that's not the case.

"Honey, I wish I had the answers for you," Lucy glances down at the other envelope Mara had left on the coffee table. "How many are there?"

"Lucas suggested there are more, if I'm willing to look."

"More." Lucy shakes her head. "Do you want to find them?"

Mara leans back and closes her eyes against the sting of tears forming. "Do I? Yes, of course I do. But…I can only take so much, you know?"

"Through it all, remember your mother loved you, Mara. I've never known someone to love with such fierceness. You were her everything. Remember that as you read these and discover things that might not make sense." Placing her hand on Mara's knee, Lucy gives it a light squeeze.

Mara's glad that Lucy's here, for her insights, for having someone here to talk things through because otherwise, she knows she'd be falling apart.

"Sometimes, that love felt suffocating," Mara admits. "Even though I didn't know it at the time." She glances at Lucy, who gives her a slight understanding nod. "I'll be honest, Lucy, right now, that love feels conflicted and manipulative."

Chapter Thirty-Two

The need to escape is strong, especially after Lucy finds another three letters hidden away in Lucas' books.

While the rest of the girls are all still relaxing in their rooms, and with Lucy somewhere in the house chatting with her father, Mara grabs the letters and journals, stuffing them in a bag, and quietly makes her way out of the house.

Being alone is exactly what she needs right now.

She sends everyone a quick text in case anyone is looking for her, that she's gone out for a walk and will be back in time for dinner, then heads aimlessly through the streets, unsure of where she's headed.

She wishes she were here under different circumstances that would enable her to enjoy getting lost within the small town, enjoying each new discovery, and breathing in the crisp air so her soul could refresh.

This trip isn't what she expected it to be. She's trying really hard to enjoy it, lose herself in the moments, and make the memories her mother wanted her to have...but honestly, she wishes she were back home instead.

A Belgium Chocolate Christmas

Instead, she's full of anxiety and questions that she's not sure she wants the answers to, not anymore.

Walking along the canal, Mara turns toward what appears to be an open market in a square center. There's a sign indicating this was once a fish market, but instead of fresh fish being sold, there are vendors for jewellery, journals, and paintings.

Mara slows her steps and stops before a man sitting at an easel. He's engrossed in his work, painting delicate strokes with a brush. His inspiration comes from the view in front of him, of a covered tunnel just up ahead.

"Hello," a gentle voice calls out.

Mara turns to find a woman standing at a table, organizing painted canvases.

"These are beautiful," Mara claims as she looks down at a watercolor painting of a canal with flowering vines climbing a building. A rowboat sits in the middle of the canal, but it's the buildings and flowers that catches Mara's attention. It reminds her of Barabas.

"This is Johannes Bourdin," the woman tells her. "He's one of our local artists and seeing him in action is a treat for you today. He only comes home to Bruges a few times a year now to paint."

"These are all his?" The table is full of his work.

"Well, of course they are. Let me know if there's anything that piques your interest."

Mara takes her time going through the paintings, pulling a few to the side that speak to her. She looks over her shoulder toward the easel, enjoying watching Johannes work.

"Have you been to Bruges before," the woman asks.

Mara shakes her head.

"What he's painting now is the arch over the Blind Donkey alley."

"Blind donkey?"

The woman smiles. "The history is that once we stole a dragon from Ghent. When they came to retrieve it, the donkey pulling the cart would not go through this alley because it was too tight. They had to blindfold the animal to get him to go through. Silly tale, if you ask me. I prefer the traditional one instead."

Intrigued, Mara stares at the alley where a beautiful archway beneath a window rests.

"It's pretty. All that gold. That's the backside to the old Recorders House. They apparently had a lot of money to waste and needed to show how important they were." The woman waves a dismissive hand toward the arch.

"You said there's a traditional tale you prefer?"

At that, a smile blooms across the woman's face. "It's an old tradition, but one the old families still keep. A young bride and groom must walk together beneath that arch for a blessed wedding. If they do, fortune will be in their future. My ex and I walked beneath that arch. The only fortune we found was when we got divorced."

Mara isn't sure whether to smile or frown, but when she notices the teasing glint in the woman's eyes, her lips turn upward.

More people arrive, and a crowd gathers around Johannes, watching him as he paints.

Before leaving, Mara ends up buying three of his watercolors. The woman rolls them up and Mara realizes she'll need to be extra careful with them bringing them home. They're too large for her suitcase but they should fit in her backpack.

The real question is where she'll place them in her house - maybe Gus would let her hang one up in the bookshop.

She takes a left from the fish market, letting her feet direct her. She could use her maps to find a park, but getting lost is all part of the journey, at least, that's what her mother always said.

Stella. A woman with so many secrets. Discovering these secrets after her death is probably normal, something most children experience as they go through their parents' belongings, but Mara has a feeling these secrets are anything but normal.

She crosses one street, then turns left at the next, and comes across a little coffee shop called Novel. Their sign is a coffee cup carved on a piece of wood, and glancing through the windows, she's drawn to walk inside.

It's like walking into someone's living room that they've converted into a little bakery. There's a fireplace in the middle of a wall, with a lounge chair and coffee table, complete with a lamp and a stack of books on top of it. Above the fireplace, instead of a large framed picture, there's a large sign of the shop's menu. Cafe tables and chairs fill up the middle space area, a long green couch fills another wall with a few cafe tables in front of it, and the back portion of the room has its bakery area.

A cute couple ahead of her in line both order hot cocoas that come with a mound of whipped cream on the side of the cup itself, and Mara has no choice but to order a cafe mocha, needing the hit of caffeine along with all that whipped cream. Before leaving, Mara heads to the coffee bar counter, adds a chocolate sauce drizzle over the cream, and then drops a coffee lid in her bag. There's no way the lid will fit until most of that cream is gone.

Once outside, ahead and to the right is a church, but before the church is a beautiful garden area where benches are strategically placed along some flower beds full of large ball ornaments and miniature Christmas trees. It's a little brisk but not too cold. She could have stayed in the coffee shop to read the rest of the letters, but she wants and needs privacy now.

She takes out the letters and journals, placing them on the bench to the side of her, but isn't quite ready to open them.

She breathes in deep, hoping for the area's tranquility to fill her soul. She needs to find some sense of peace, or even a little bit of… understanding isn't the right word, maybe acceptance to a past she should have been aware of but never knew.

Or does she?

Does knowing about the romance between her mother and father matter?

Will finding out more about Julian make a difference in her life?

Deep down, she knows the answer.

No.

Finding out the truth, making sense of her mother's words and memories, discovering the truth about her lineage, and that there's a ready-made family in her life, ultimately, it doesn't matter.

Would it be nice to know? Sure. But she's also aware that the more she discovers, the more questions she will have, and she knows those questions won't get answered.

Not by Lucy. Not by Bram. Not by Lucas.

Even if her mother was still alive, she doubts even Stella would tell her everything.

Stella had a way of only saying what was necessary, of only giving out enough information to keep one moving in a forward direction.

Even her letters prove that.

It takes a bit, but she finally comes to terms with the truth, and while it's a hard swallow of acceptance, the kernel of it takes root in her heart. She might not be able to fully accept and embrace that she'll never know the full truth right now, but one day, she will.

With a feeling of resolve, Mara reaches for her father's journals.

Learning more about him is fascinating. It's like reading a story and experiencing life through a character's point of view. There's a disconnect between her and Julian, which isn't surprising. She's plopped in the middle of his life, reading about the death of his dreams, how he feels duty-bound to stay at home and help his father rather than go off to college and teach English, a dream he's always had. He writes about his struggles to write a novel, how he doesn't feel worthy enough to pen an epic love story between characters when his own love story came to a glorious disaster, one he didn't understand.

His regret for not having a way to contact her mother is clear. He writes about his confusion about her quick departure, how she didn't even wait to say goodbye. He left one morning with her kiss on his lips and came home with instructions to tidy up her room for their next guest to arrive.

There was no goodbye. No whispered words of love and longing for a future together.

Reading the emotional rollercoaster he'd been on is hard. It's so visceral that she can feel his pain, his confusion, his heartbreak.

She looks at the dates of his journal entries, and then the dates of her mother's letters to him.

If only Lucas had shared the letters, how different would her life be?

There are so many what ifs, should haves, could haves, would haves when it comes to all of this, that it's a dangerous game to play.

If she goes down that road, her anger is directed at Lucas because he's the one who caused all this heartache.

But she can't ignore that her mother kept all of this from her, either.

She lied for years, even to the point of having her draw pictures for a father she never knew and saying they were for Santa.

The only truly innocent party in this threesome of pain is her father.

They were young lovers. They were also young parents. What would it have been like to be raised by him? To have him in her life? How different would things have been?

Guess that's one more question that will never be answered.

Chapter Thirty-Three

After about an hour on the bench, Mara heads back to The Novel and is thankful not to find it overflowing with customers. Her phone is blowing up with messages from the others. Kat found a chocolate and brandy tasting for tonight, and Jo-Jo wants another round of the market in the main square for last-minute photos. They have a few more days left in Bruges, but they are filled with day trips to Ghent and Antwerp, along with stops in a few other small towns along the way.

Thinking about staying longer, about going to those towns and the markets, only fills Mara with dread instead of excitement. She's ready for this trip to be over, ready to go home and return to her normal, regular life.

She does a quick search for return flights, finds one that leaves tomorrow night, and then quickly closes the browser before she does anything rash.

She orders another mocha, finds a table off in the corner, takes out her headphones, and video calls Nenita, not even looking at the time difference between them.

They chat for a little bit before Mara opens up and blurts out everything that's been happening.

"Okay, let me get this straight," Nenita leans back in her chair and runs her fingers through her hair. "You get a letter from your mother's deathbed telling you to go to Belgium and enjoy the markets, but the reality is she wants you to meet your father's side of the family, except she doesn't want you to consider them family, she just wants you to know the truth. You find out about your father, think that he knew all about you but didn't want you - except, he didn't know about you after all, and when he did finally find out the truth, on his way to the airport to come to see you and he dies. Fast forward years, and on a chance trip, Lucy shows up in Paris and sees your mother, then learns about you, and in the midst of all that, she declares her father dead to her and dedicates her life to being a part of yours. Did I miss anything?" Nenita is out of breath as she completes her recap.

"You missed the part about finding letters I doubt my father ever read, and all the pictures I drew," Mara says.

"Right...because that's what you do when you get letters in the mail for people, you hide them in old stuffy books no one will ever read. I'm sorry...like, who does that?" Nenita glances off to the side of the screen and Mara wonders if Chris is there, listening in. It's okay if he is.

"Lucas, apparently. From what I gathered, he does it all the time now. Bram says he finds invoices and menus and even pamphlets all over the place."

"He's sick, right? Like physically not doing well?"

"Yeah. I guess the doctors only give him four more months or something. He has some cancer that he's refuses treatment for. And his memory isn't the best. I think early onset dementia, but Bram won't say anything about it."

"Weird, right? I mean, I get it, people like to keep secrets within the family, but you are now part of that family."

Mara shakes her head. "I'm not ready for that type of relationship yet. On that, Mom was right. Lucas might be related to me by blood, but that doesn't mean I have to embrace him as my grandfather."

"You sound pretty sure about that."

Mara inhales and takes a moment to consider the question. "It feels right," she says, tapping her chest, "in here. He won't even apologize, did I mention that?"

"Seriously?"

Mara glances around the room, remembering she's not alone. "He says what's done is done, and there's no going back. That apologies are meant for the people issuing them, to cleanse their own guilt and grief, and do nothing for the ones truly affected by their choices and actions."

She understands what he's saying but doesn't completely agree with using that as an excuse.

"Okay, but...come on. A sincere *I'm sorry for making your mother leave and for ignoring you for your whole life* seems like something one would do, don't you think?"

An apology would be nice, but at this point, it's a little too late and wouldn't change anything.

"And yet, the guy created a museum for you, so that has to say something."

"Something about his guilt, maybe?" Mara doesn't even know what to do with all that. Sure, it means that somewhere deep down, Lucas feels a lot of regret for what he did, but that excuses nothing.

"So, what are you going to do?" Nenita asks, not waiting for an answer. "Are you staying there? Or will you leave and travel someplace else?"

Mara can't help but smile. Her friend knows her too well.

"I think I'm going to come home. Too much has happened for me to enjoy going somewhere by myself."

Nenita nods. "Yeah, I get that. The others won't mind, will they?"

Mara shakes her head. "I don't think so."

"What about Lucy?"

Lucy might be the only one to have an issue with her leaving.

"Honestly, I have no idea. I mean...I mentioned we should leave, but she refused to consider the option. I think she should stay here for a while. Reconnect with Bram and help out with Lucas. I mean if he only has a few months left..." Mara lets her voice drop off.

"Yeah. I don't even know what to say about that. I mean...after all these years, to go back home and discover your only surviving parent is dying...damn, that's rough."

Rough probably doesn't describe Lucy's feelings, but then she wouldn't know either. Lucy's been tight-lipped about everything.

"She's been off since we got here, that's for sure," Mara admits.

"Off? Girl, I'd be medicating with wine every night if I was being forced to face a past like that."

"Hey, wifey, who are you talking to?" Chris, Nenita's husband, comes into view on the screen. "Oh hey, shortie, how is...where are you again?" He bends down, face filling the camera screen until it's all she sees.

"Love seeing your face, but that's a little too much, you know?" Mara says, leaning back by habit.

"What? You don't like looking at this mug? I know my wifey sure does." He plants a loud, smack-type kiss on Nenita's face before he laughs. "Where are you again? Running around the..." his lips purse as he glances around. "What's that thing on the wall called?" He points off-camera, confusion, and frustration evident on his face.

"Globe, honey."

He sighs. "Running around the globe. Where are you?" He sounds like he's lost interest in the conversation, but he's trying to keep up the facade.

"I'm in Belgium, but I'll be coming home soon," Mara says. "And I'm bringing back chocolate."

"You sure know the way to a man's heart, don't you? I knew there was a reason we liked this girl."

He walks away, and Mara hears his opening cupboards and closing them again before his shuffling feet go off into the distance.

"How's he doing?" Mara asks once she's sure he can't hear her.

Nenita shrugs. "He has his good days and bad. Today's an okay one. He's losing more words every day, though, and that's hard. I'm adding more labels to things around the house for him."

Mara feels for her friend, wishing there is something she can do to help her.

"We're going back to those classes in the city starting next week," Nenita says. "It'll be good for Chris. They'll teach him other ways to keep his mind active and help me in being his caregiver."

"Is there anything I can do?"

"You, a hug, and that chocolate you're bringing home is all I need, girlfriend. Don't you be worrying about me, you hear? We know what's happening, we know the end game, it's just a matter of staying the course, remaining strong, and taking each day as it comes."

"I love you," Mara says.

"I know you do. I love you back. I'm sorry for this crazy trip you've had and all the info that's come to light. Your mother...I wish she'd done this a long time ago, you know?"

"You and me both. I'm not getting the complete picture, and it's aggravating."

"I doubt you ever will, as sad as that is."

"I know. There's a flight leaving tomorrow night. I can't do this anymore, and I don't care if that makes me sound calloused or not." Now that she's said it, she knows it's the right decision. "This is all too much, and to be honest, it's a rabbit hole I don't care to go down."

Nenita nods. "Send me your flight details, and we'll come pick you up."

"Am I doing the right thing?" She's not sure why she asked because she knows she is.

Nenita hesitates, and a look on her face causes Mara to have a moment of self-doubt.

"I don't think there's a right or wrong way to handle this, hun. Being there is forcing a relationship that you don't even know if you want. Some space and time might be prudent. And if you need or want to, you can always go back for a visit. I think if you feel overwhelmed and unsure, then you need to listen to that."

Mara bites her lip as she thinks about her friend's words. Nenita is right - there is no right or wrong way to deal with this. She needs to go with her gut.

"I'll send you the details once I've changed my flight."

Nenita nods. "Sounds good. Just remember one thing, okay? Your mother wasn't perfect, but if there was one thing she was perfect in, it was loving you."

Chapter Thirty-Four

"You did what?" Lucy stands there, arms crossed over her chest, with the fiercest frown she's ever seen, on her face.

"It's already done. My flight leaves tomorrow night." Mara swallows hard but stands her ground. This is the right decision, she knows it. It's the right decision for her.

Lucy heaves a very long sigh but eventually drops her arms to her side. "I guess I'm not surprised. This has all been a little much."

Mara nods before she drops into a chair and looks at her luggage.

"I almost wish I was going home with you, but I think I'll stay here a little longer instead," Lucy says. "While the others head on their day trips, I'll stay here with Bram and Dad."

A flash of sadness flitters through Lucy's gaze. "Being here is probably the right thing. Especially now…" She heads toward the window and pulls back the curtain. "I never thought I'd come back here, you know? I knew one day he'd pass away, but I…well, I'm glad I'm here, I guess." One hand fists tight around the fabric. "He doesn't have much time, and as frustrating as he is, I'm glad I'm here."

Lucy finally turns and looks at her. "He won't say it, but I know he regrets everything."

A seed of anger sprouts inside Mara, and rather than squash it like she probably should, she lets it grow, just a tiny little bit.

"What exactly do you think he regrets, Lucy?" Mara asks her. "Regrets forcing my mom to leave and keep me a secret? Regrets hiding the letters from mom for so long? Regrets being the reason my father left here in a hurry and was probably driving too fast because of whatever he was feeling? Regrets never contacting Mom and welcoming me into his life? Regrets losing you? What, Lucy? What exactly do you think he regrets?" She lets the words fly, the anger mount, the frustration seep over into her very being.

There is no way to excuse the truth of what happened. No possible way. It doesn't matter if times were different, or if the Flemish culture is different to her Canadian one, or that choices were made she will never understand. There is no excuse for what Lucas did.

There's also no excuse for what her mother did, either. For keeping this family a secret from her.

"I understand the anger," Lucy says, leaving her post at the window and sitting down on the couch.

"I'm sorry," Mara leans forward, resting her elbows on her knees. "I'm not angry with you. Well, I kind of am, I guess. You kept all of this a secret, too. You're as bad as Stella, and she's the one I'm truly angry with."

Lucy nods, dropping her gaze. "Would it help if I said I'd do things differently if I could?"

Mara shakes her head. "No, because that doesn't help, does it?"

"You're right. All I can do is say I'm sorry because I truly am, Mara. I am so, so sorry."

Mara hears the truth in her words and takes them to heart. It might be the only apology she receives from this family, and it is enough. It's enough because Lucy is her family, and family should always be willing to forgive.

"You are my family, Lucy," Mara gets up from her chair and joins Lucy on the couch, placing her arm around the older woman's waist. "That will never change. Mom once told me that families will always hurt each other, but in the end, we'll always forgive, too. We might not forget, but we shouldn't either. Forgetting means pretending things didn't happen, and that's not something I'm willing to do. We forgive, we don't forget, but we learn and grow and don't repeat those same hurts." She leans her head down on Lucy's shoulder. "I love you. We'll be stronger after all of this."

When she lifts her head, it's to see tears streaking down Lucy's face.

"I love you, too, girl," Lucy says as she takes a tissue from the sleeve of her sweater and wipes her eyes.

Mara glances at the time. "Are you joining us tonight?" They all agreed to meet outside in about ten minutes. She hears chatter out in the hallway and realizes a few of the girls are already ready.

Lucy shakes her head. "Today's a good day for Lucas, and Bram says there aren't many of them. He's made Lucas' favorite meal, and I figure now is as good a time as any to heal some old wounds. I'll see you when you get back."

Mara wraps a scarf around her neck and then shrugs on her jacket. "I'll see you later then."

Mara keeps her news to herself until the chocolate and brandy tasting. Everyone was in such a good mood over dinner, excited to head to Ghent, that she didn't want to ruin the mood. The news of her leaving is best served with a piece of chocolate and a sip of alcohol.

She waits until they're all relaxed after their little tasting, sitting in a cute alcove in a closed restaurant, enjoying the last samples of chocolate and brandy.

"Guys, I'm going to head home tomorrow."

"What? Why?" Kat immediately leans close and grabs her arm. "What's going on?"

A Belgium Chocolate Christmas

"We only have a few days left, Mara, don't go, please," Jo-Jo grabs her other arm and gives a pretty pout.

"I already changed my flight. My train leaves close to yours tomorrow, so we can say goodbye at the train station." She keeps a firm resolve in her voice, not leaving any room for discussion. "With everything that's happening, it's all a little overwhelming."

"What do you mean?" Donna asks as she breaks a piece of chocolate in two. "What else has happened?

She realizes the girls are on the outside of all the news, so she fills them in, sharing how she met Lucas, the letters he hid, the room with her childhood drawings, her father's journals...she doesn't leave anything out.

At first, no one says anything. She tries to read the thoughts on their faces, but it's hard in the dim lighting.

"I'm sorry," Sandra says, the first to speak up, "and this might hurt, but I'm sincerely pissed with your mother right now. If she were still here, we'd be having words."

"If she were still here, this wouldn't be happening," I say softly, correcting her.

"I'm with Sandra on this," Kat says. "I'm not too thrilled with Lucy right now, either. She knew, and she could have said something."

Everyone nods.

"I get it," Jo-Jo says. "I'd want to go home too. That's safety. It's comfortable and easier to digest everything instead of staying here, right in the middle of things. I mean...considering where we're staying and everything, it's not like you have much space to get away from it all and really take it in."

Whatever heaviness Mara wore on her shoulders lifts as her friends understand. Deep down, she knew they would.

"Don't blame Lucy," she pleads with them all. "Mom was a force; we all know that."

The skepticism on all their faces says they don't fully agree with her.

"Lucy is a force all on her own, though. This explains so much, looking back. The connection between the two seemed so sudden, but I guess it wasn't. It was steeped in history and cemented in a bond that not even time could break." Kat quirks her lips as her gaze rests solely on Mara.

Mara squirms in her seat under the intensity of her look.

"Are you and Lucy okay?"

Sandra asks the question, but Mara knows everyone else is thinking it, too.

She nods. "I'm not going to lie, it's a little rough right now. Knowing she kept this a secret, it hurts. But does it change anything? I've always considered her family, and with how close she and Mom were, she's always been a constant presence in my life. Knowing we're truly family only makes it official." She shrugs as she holds her brandy glass in her hand.

"What about Lucas and Bram, though? They're family, too, and she kept them from you." Sandra nudges in the only way Sandra can, with a sweetness in her voice that masks the harshness of her question.

"Does that mean we have to be close? Do I have to embrace them right away? Or can it be a slow acceptance after I've had time to digest everything? I mean...sure, Lucas is old and dying, and I sympathize with Lucy that she's losing a parental figure, but he's also the same man who kept me from my father, who forced my mother to run, who never reached out or acknowledged me. Am I supposed to forgive all that in an instant and embrace him as my grandfather?"

The question is genuine and sincere, and she'd love to have these women give some insight because, as far as she's concerned, the expectation of all of that is too much for her.

"Honey," Donna speaks up as she pushes her own cup around the table in circles. "Family is who you choose to have in your life. Just because someone is related by blood, doesn't mean they get access to your heart." Her focus is on the cup, and Mara doesn't miss the way she won't look at anyone as she speaks. "I've never really told you all this, but I didn't have the best upbringing. There was a lot of...abuse...in my family when I was a child, and I ended up being raised by a distant aunt. That was probably the best thing that could have happened to me, truth be told. It also probably saved my life. My parents are both dead, you know that, but what you don't know is that I never went to their funerals, much less spoke to them my whole adult life."

The stunned silence among the group is deafening.

"I'm so sorry." Sandra is the first to speak.

"I can't even imagine what your life was like," Jo-Jo is close to tears. "I'm so sorry, hun."

Donna waves her hand dismissively. "I didn't say that for your sympathy. I said it to help Mara understand that family by blood and family by choice are very different, and they don't have to be the same."

Mara can't speak. Anything she might want to say is enclosed in a bubble of grief lodged in her throat. Donna may be the quietest of the group, but her presence has always been felt. She's the quiet mother hen, who keeps extra tissues in her purse, who brings extra mitts and scarves, who makes sure everyone's coffee is ordered before they arrive at the table. She's the one who sends out personal emails making sure everyone is okay, and she was the one who sent Mara a care package after Stella's death, even slipping her some local gift cards and making sure her freezer was stuffed with frozen meals from a local shop in Canmore.

"Thank you," Mara is finally able to squeeze out. The tears are in her voice, and they don't go unnoticed. "Thank you for not only sharing that but also for the reminder. I love you all, so very much, and when I think of family, you ladies are mine."

Chapter Thirty-Five

"Leaving without notice seems to run in the family," Bram says as he hands Mara a coffee the following morning. "I can't believe you are leaving now, after all this. I've wanted to meet you for a long time, to get to know you."

"Then why didn't you?" Mara knows her words are cutting, but after a sleepless night of late-night chats with Lucy and then all the tossing and turning, there's no energy for any other emotion this morning.

"My father and the B&B...which, to you, probably sound like excuses."

"A little." Mara has no energy for anything other than honesty this morning. She came down early so she could say goodbye before the rest of the group joined them. "You always knew how to get in touch with me, I mean, it's not like you lost complete contact with Lucy, right?"

He sighs and has the decency to at least look embarrassed at being caught.

"You remind me so much of your mother, especially now. She didn't let people take the easy road either."

"Well, I am my mother's daughter." And very proud of it too.

"Lucas, he enjoyed meeting you yesterday."

Mara nods, unsure of how to respond. She can't really claim the same.

"My father has always been a complicated man who was raised in a generation that was taught emotions had to be stuffed and hidden."

"And I have been raised in a generation where we know that's a complete crock."

Bram nods, giving her a slight smile. "That may be true, but the gap between our generation and his is sometimes too wide of a gap. I stopped trying to explain or even understand his methods."

Mara sips her coffee, looking at Bram over the brim of her cup. "You're a man full of excuses, they must come naturally to you."

He winces, but she doesn't feel the need to apologize.

"So where does that leave us?" He waves his hand between the two of them. "Mistakes have been made, but we are family, and I don't want to lose that."

She wants to tell him this isn't up to him anymore, that he had his chance and blew it, but she can also hear her mother telling her to be the better person, to pick her battles, and be honest about her motives.

Right now, she's tired. Tired of the emotional rollercoaster she's been on since finding out about this trip - a trip she wishes she'd never come on.

"Honestly, I don't know. Maybe we exchange Christmas and birthday cards, send email updates, and just take this slow."

"Slow," Bram says, drawing out the word, nodding his head as if accepting the idea. "If that's what you need, then I'll respect that. I can see if I can find more of Julian's stuff and send them to you. It's only right, as his daughter."

Daughter. She swallows hard. She was a daughter to two people who are now deceased. She's a daughter without parents to explain their past actions, their history together, and what it meant to be separated by force.

"I know my father won't apologize, but I want to," Bram says.

Mara remains silent. Lucy had said the same yesterday. Sadly, their apologizing for Lucas really doesn't mean much to her.

"You're right," Bram continues. "I should have reached out. Once Lucy told me about you, I should have put you first and tried to get to know you."

"But then Lucy would have had to tell me who she was, and she didn't. I didn't know until we got here."

He nods. "There is that. My sister didn't make it easy. She told me of her promise to your mother, and I guess, it was easier for me to respect that. Right or wrong, it's the truth."

Mara understands, she really does. It's still hard to hear. Still hard to process.

"I need some time to process the past before I can think about our future, okay? I'm not locking the door, just closing it for a moment of reprieve."

Bram swallows hard, but she sees the acceptance on his face as they hear the thump-thump-thump of footsteps coming down the front staircase.

"Guess that's my signal to get your breakfast started." Bram tosses a cloth over his shoulder and grabs a tray.

"Ahh, you're up," Jo-Jo says as they all enter the kitchen. "When we didn't hear from you this morning, we all figured you were sleeping in."

"And miss our last breakfast together, I don't think so." Mara grabs her coffee and joins them as they head toward the breakfast nook. Bram set up a large table for them, complete with two silver trays full of chocolate eggs, cut fruit, freshly baked pastries, and slices of cheese and meat.

"I'm really going to miss this type of breakfast," Mara says as she grabs one of the chocolate eggs and breaks it with her spoon.

"You're just going to miss the excuse of having chocolate during your first meal," Kat teases her as she, too, takes a chocolate egg and breaks it apart.

Together, they stuff the largest piece into their mouths and giggle like schoolgirls.

"This will now be our breakfast at home. No more huge meals and bowls of sugary cereal," Jo-Jo proclaims like she's royalty.

"I don't know. I kind of like my big bowl of chocolate cereal in the mornings, or even as a late-night snack. The best part is drinking the chocolate milk afterward," Mara says.

"Well, there is that." One side of Jo-Jo's lips tilt upward in a half smile. "Maybe the cereal could be saved for the weekends."

The rest of their breakfast is spent chatting about getting ready for the holidays once they're all back home, with Jo-Jo reminding everyone of the champagne kit coming their way.

Lucy doesn't join until later, when they're all sitting at the table sipping their last cups of coffee.

"Good morning, ladies," she says as she pulls out a chair. "Sorry, I'm late."

Lucy looks beyond exhausted, with dark circles beneath her eyes and the slump of her shoulders as she holds her cup in her hands. There's a heavy weight that encompasses her whole being and for Mara, it's hard to see.

"We're sorry about your father," Sandra says, leaning forward and lightly touching Lucy's hand.

Lucy only nods while she stares at the tablecloth.

"I know you all have feelings about what's happened since we've arrived and all the secrets that have been revealed. Just like I know you all have feelings about my part in it—"

"Stop." Kat interrupts her. "Whatever you're about to say, it's not necessary. We all make decisions based on a plethora of choices available to us, and the ones you made were the right ones for you at that time. We're all very sorry for what you must be going through right now, though, and I want you to remember this one thing, Lucy. You are not alone. Okay? We love you and have your back."

Lucy nods, large teardrops dangling from her lashes.

"We all love you," Mara adds softly, taking Lucy's hand in hers and giving it a hard squeeze.

Their chat last night had been hard for both of them. A lot of honest words were spoken from both sides, along with a lot of healing.

"I'm going to stay here, if you all don't mind, while you spend your last few days at the markets. I need to be here, at least for now," Lucy says. She glances toward the kitchen, where Bram is whistling. "I cut myself off from my brother and father and didn't fully realize what I'd missed until coming back here."

"As long as you'll sit with us when we get back and listen to all our stories," Jo-Jo says. "I expect we'll be needing large mugs of strong mochas to warm us up."

Lucy smiles. "I think that can be arranged."

Mara glances at her watch and realizes the time. "Um, I hate to break up the party, but I need to get going if I'm going to make my train."

"Bram has offered his vehicle," Lucy says. "He's going to bring it around to the alley for us."

With quick hugs and last-minute goodbyes, Mara rushes upstairs to grab her bags, once again thankful she only brought carry-ons.

Both Bram and Lucas are at the door, waiting for her.

"This isn't the last you'll be hearing from us," Bram says as he places her bags in the back of his car.

"I hope it's not." Mara gives him a quick hug and then turns to Lucas, unsure of what to say or do.

He looks frail and tired, and she can see the effort it is taking for him to stand there. They stand in silence, measuring each other up, working up the courage to be the first to say something.

Lucas holds out a bag. "It's not much, but will you take this home with you?" Without waiting for a reply, he enfolds her in a surprisingly tight hug. "I missed out on one of the best things about getting old. Having a grandchild to love." He whispers in her ear. "I hope you'll forgive me."

Mara wraps her arms around him, knowing this will be the last time she sees him. She memorizes the feel of being in his arms, imagining this might have been what it would have felt like to be hugged by her father.

"Of course, I do," Mara says softly, letting the healing from those words take root in her heart and soul. Forgiveness doesn't mean forgetting, but it does mean letting go. Letting go is also a process, but one she's willing to start.

Chapter Thirty-Six

Mara-mine,

The words I love you hold so much power and meaning.
I wish I had more time to say them to you. I wish I'd said them more often.
Of all the things I have done with my life, you are my greatest treasure and accomplishment.
I've always called you my Christmas baby. You were born early, so you're more like my birthday baby, but you are still my gift and one I have always treasured.
From the moment I knew of you, I knew you would change my life for the better. Everything I gave up, everything I sacrificed, everything I did...it was all for you.
I wasn't perfect. I won't even try to pretend that I was. I made mistakes - a lot of them. I made choices for you that, looking back, weren't the best for you. I have a lot of regrets, but there is one thing I will never regret.
I will never regret you. I will never regret having you, loving you, raising you.

You are everything I hoped I could have been. You are the best of me, Mara.

Life hasn't always been easy for us - especially the last few years. I know I haven't been particularly easy, either. Blame it on the disease. Blame it on my stubbornness. Regardless of the reason, I want you to know how much I appreciate that you have stood by me, loving me even at my worst.

I want you to do something for me, sweet daughter.

I want you to live your best life from this moment forward. I need you to. You need you to.

Don't live in the past. Don't let the secrets I kept dictate your future. Don't let the hiccups of my unforgiveness and stubbornness affect your choices.

Family is what you make it out to be. Family is who you choose to let close to your heart. Make those choices for yourself, not based on my fears, okay, sweetheart?

You are amazing, Mara. You are strong and confident, beautiful, and resilient. But most of all, you are loved by many, and don't ever forget that.

Although, no one will love you more than me. It's just not possible.

Forever on your side, always by your side,
Mom

Chapter Thirty-Seven

WEEKS LATER

With a glass of champagne in one hand and a macaron in the other, Mara smiles into the camera as she listens to Jo-Jo share news of her holiday escapades in New York. Party after party, followed by ice skating and listening to choirs, it all sounds fun and chaotic at the same time.

"I said all that to say this...I think you should all come to New York next year," Jo-Jo finishes. "A friend of mine has already agreed to let you stay at their place while they spend the holidays in the Maldives, so that will save on hotel costs and guys, it's the most gorgeous brownstone you've ever seen. I swear. Plus, it's close to Central Park."

"New York at Christmas, who can say no?" Kat says.

Donna slowly raises her hand. "Me."

"What?" Jo-Jo leans forward. "You're turning down my holiday suggestion?" A pout graces her lips. "Don't you like New York? You've always said how fun it would be during Christmas, and we'll even do a Broadway show..."

Full regret shows on Donna's face. "I know, and if it were any other time, I'd be there in a heartbeat, but Lola really wants to go to London during the holidays, and since it's not on our Europe year, I don't feel like I can say no. She's been saving her money, and you know I promised all the girls one trip of their choice."

"Well, if it's because of Lola, then that's okay," Jo-Jo says, removing her pout. "She's going to love London. We've never actually spent time there, have we? I mean, we had that layover fiasco this last trip when we had twelve hours in London, but that was a whirlwind of a visit."

"Hey, has anyone heard from Lucy? Mara?" Sandra pipes up. "Sorry, totally off topic, but..."

Mara nods. "We just spoke earlier today. She says hi and sends her love. Her husband flew over to spend Christmas in Belgium with her, which you all know. He's still there for a few more days - I guess he's leaving after New Year's, and she'll stay a little longer. Lucas isn't doing well, and she doesn't think he has another month."

Sharing that news is hard. She glances over at the gifts Lucas gave her as she was leaving Bruges. That Christmas tree drawing she'd found on the wall, including one of the black sheep figures from his bookshelf. Since returning home, Mara has had the space to think and let herself process everything. Over the weeks, she's been slowly building relationships with Bram and Lucas, and it's been nice. Lucas can't talk much, but when he has good days, Lucy always sends her a message asking if she'd be up to a video chat with Lucas. She has yet to say no.

She doesn't regret leaving early, and while connecting with Lucas has been nice, she's still grieving losing her mother. Focusing on herself, her healing...even though the timing sucks, she knows it is the right thing to do. Bram suggested he may visit in late spring for a week or so. He'd love to see the mountains and explore the rugged outdoors of Banff National Park. Mara suggested he come in the summer during the Calgary Stampede, the largest outdoor show in the world, but he's almost fully booked for the summer, and that's not a great time for him to leave the bed and breakfast.

"So Donna is a no. I know Lucy will love the idea," Jo-Jo says, returning the focus of the conversation back to her. "What about the rest of you? Christmas in New York? I promise to make it amazing."

A text pops up with a message from Nenita.

Chris and I are outside. We've got a thermos full of hot cocoa you brought home. Come for a drive to see the lights with us.

Mara can't help but smile.

"Oh...I see that look," Kat says. "Mara, what's going on?"

She glances at her phone, then at the screen, and makes her decision. "Sorry guys, I need to run early. Nenita and her husband are outside, and I guess we're going on a drive to view all the Christmas lights. Again."

This will be the fourth time she's gone for a drive with them to see the lights. It's one of Chris' favorite things to do, and every drive is like his first one of the season.

"Go ahead. We'll miss you, but chat next month, okay?"

Mara blows them all kisses, then closes out of the chat.

On my way! She grabs her jacket, a new scarf Lily knitted for her as a holiday gift, and then laces up her boots.

Once outside, she can hear Christmas music blasting from their truck. Nenita is behind the wheel, and Chris has a look of excitement on his face.

"Hop in girly. It's time to see all the lights. This will be our new tradition, okay?" He holds out a cup with steaming cocoa to her. "We're going to end the night at Gus and Lily's. Lily made cookies and Gus needs help setting up a new outdoor Santa scene."

"I'm all about starting new traditions," Mara says. This is her fourth time saying it, but she doesn't mind.

This is her family. Chris and Nenita. Gus and Lily. Lucy and the girls. She was worried about feeling alone, about the holidays not feeling the same without Stella. She wasn't wrong, things are different, there's a different vibe, a different feel without her mother there. But the love is there. The love hasn't changed, and that's what matters in the end.

Chris turns up the volume as his favorite Christmas song plays.

"It's not my last Christmas..." he belts out, changing the words, adding his own, as he looks back at Mara with a wink. "And look, I gave you that cup...."

She laughs, then joins in, singing the correct words but a tad softer so she doesn't miss out on his take.

* * *

Dear reader,

Thank you for reading the first book in my Tinsel Travelers Series! I hope you enjoyed the complicated relationship between Mara and Lucy...don't worry, you'll be seeing more of them!

Book 2 will focus on Donna and her daughter Lola as they head to London, UK and spend some quality mother/daughter time exploring the markets there. Nothing could go wrong, right? Sometimes simple mother/daughter trips are anything but simple...

Be sure to follow me on social media or join my newsletter for all future release updates! As a special thank you for joining my mail list, please download a free book from me to you...so head to www.steenaholmes.com for more information!

Happy Reading...
Steena

A Personal Note

Did you know...

In 2019, I hosted my first Reader Trip as we took a river cruise to explore the Christmas Markets, starting off in Amsterdam and ending in Basel, Switzerland. During that trip, my family and I explored Amsterdam and then took the train to Brussels, where we stayed in the core and walked through the markets. My husband and I found this adorable whiskey setup and were excited to discover maple whiskey for the first time! (I'm a huge fan, my husband-not so much, it's too sweet for him...go figure).

All the chocolate shops listed in Brussels were shops I'd personally visited during our time there!

In 2023, I hosted another Reader Trip, this one was a river cruise again and we explored Amsterdam and Belgium, with the focus being on chocolate. Knowing I wanted to write a book that focused on chocolate and Bruges, I came early and stayed in the Barabas B&B. Sadly, I didn't take Stella's advice and brought a larger suitcase I had to lug around. Trust me, when you have to jump from one train to another, you instantly regret not packing lighter! Thankfully, I didn't break any wheels on this trip, but I have in the past.

A Personal Note

The tree on the tracks, the family in the train station in Brussels, the rain and muddy sidewalk in Amsterdam, and even the fantastic apple pie are all things I experienced. If you ever get a chance to do a Chocolate-In-The-Dark experience, do it! My description within the story doesn't do the experience justice - so if you ever get the opportunity, do it, I promise you won't regret it!

I love the Christmas Markets and since I've always wanted to do a series with the markets as the backdrop, I knew this would be the perfect story to start with! I can't wait to write more of the books...book 2 will be set in London during the holidays, Book 3 will be in Paris...every Tinsel Traveler in the group will have their own book - exciting, right?

Plus, who doesn't love European Christmas Markets! There's something about them that feels magical and as I host more Christmas Market Reader Tours, I hope that one day you'll be able to join me! If you're interested - head on over to my website - all the info on my upcoming tours is there!

About the Author

Who am I? I'm just a girl addicted to chocolate, travel, reading and my fur babies (I share too many photos on Instagram of them, I know...but...they're just so cute and they love to hang with me while I write).

I love to write stories that deal with family secrets and how those secrets affect lives. I also love to add chocolate, coffee, and other personal passions into my stories (like travel and Christmas Markets set in Europe).

Speaking of travel...I love going on trips and started 'reader trips' where you can come with me as we explore Europe and more!

You're probably wondering where have we gone / where are we going? Well, we've done a Christmas Market River Cruise in Europe, a Sweet Tour of Paris, a Chocolate & Tulips River Cruise, we're headed to the Amalfi Coast, and of course, you have to join me for my Sweet Christmas in Paris tour!

If you want more info...join my newsletter or find me in my Steena Travels FB group. I'd love to travel with you!

Now onto the official bio...
Official Bio:
New York Times & USA Today Bestselling Author!
With close to 3 million copies of her titles sold worldwide, Steena Holmes was named in the Top 20 Women Author to read

in 2015 by Good Housekeeping. She continues to write books that deal with issues that deal with secrets, whether it is through her contemporary fiction or psychological suspense novels.

To find out more about her books and her love for traveling, you can visit her website at http://www.steenaholmes.com

2012 NATIONAL INDIE EXCELLENCE BOOK Award for her bestselling novel Finding Emma

2015 USA BOOK NEWS Award for The Word Game,

2015 USA BOOK NEWS finalist for The Memory Child.

Instagram: www.instagram.com/steenaholmes

Facebook: SteenaHolmes.author

Twitter: @steenaholmes

Email: steena@steenaholmes.com

For softer, sweeter stories with a touch of romance mixed in with a hint of chocolate, a lot of coffee, and communities you want to live in, look for her stories under the name STEENA MARIE.

DON'T MISS THE FOLLOWING NOVELS:

WOMENS FICTION
Finding Emma
Emma's Secret
The Memory Child
Stillwater Rising
The Word Game
Saving Abby
Abby's Journey

PSYCHOLOGICAL SUSPENSE/THRILLERS
The Forgotten Ones
The Patient
Engaged to a Serial Killer
The Sister Under the Stairs
The Twin

HOLIDAY NOVELS
Second Chances at the Chocolate Blessings Cafe
The Promise of Christmas
The Halfway Series - start with Halfway to Nowhere

facebook.com/authorsteenaholmes
x.com/steenaholmes
instagram.com/authorsteenaholmes